HANDS-ON AMERICA
VOLUME I

ART ACTIVITIES ABOUT VIKINGS, WOODLAND INDIANS AND EARLY COLONISTS

This book is dedicated to a colleague and friend of nearly thirty years. Mary Simpson and I first met in Anchorage, Alaska when we produced a youth exhibit on Shape as an Element in Art in 1976. We have been producing educational kits, exhibits and books since then. Mary has an extraordinary talent, an exemplary character and is cherished as a friend.

Book design by Art & International Productions, LLC, Anchorage, Alaska
Laurel Casjens took the photographs.
Mary Simpson illustrated the book and assisted with the development of the crafts
and the research on the Indian unit.
Madlyn Tanner edited and proofread the text.

Books by the author
from KITS Publishing:

Hands-on Africa
(ISBN 0-9643177-7-X)

Hands-on Alaska
(ISBN 0-9643177-3-7)

Hands-on American Vol. I
(ISBN 0-9643177-6-1)

Hands-on Asia
(ISBN 0-9643177-5-3)

Hands-on Celebrations
(ISBN 0-9643177-4-5)

Hands-on Rocky Mountains
(ISBN 0-9643177-2-9)

Hands-on Latin America
(ISBN 0-9643177-1-0)

Hands-on Pioneers*
(ISBN 1-57345-085-5)

KITS PUBLISHING
2359 E. Bryan Avenue Salt Lake City, Utah 84108
(801) 582-2517   fax: (801) 582-2540
e-mail - info@hands-on.com web - www.hands-on.com
*Published by Deseret Book

© 2001 Yvonne Young Merrill
First printing August, 2001
Printed in China
All rights reserved
Library of Congress Control Number: 2001092322
ISBN 0-9643177-6-1

Students in the title page photograph are Willie Richards, Lily and Anna Ratliff, Emma Beilfus, Daniel Sathiyanathan, Dustin Palmer, Melissa Powell, Raahil Madhok, Li Su, Ian Crossett, David Lawrence, Megan Lazarakis, Sarah Charles, Elliott Bullock and Stuart Howe. They are students at Beacon Heights Elementary School in Salt Lake City. A special thank-you to Stephanie Woodland, their teacher.

HANDS-ON
AMERICA
VOLUME I

ART ACTIVITIES ABOUT VIKINGS, WOODLAND INDIANS AND EARLY COLONISTS

Yvonne Y. MerrilL

KITS PUBLISHING

TABLE OF CONTENTS

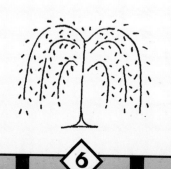

THE HANDS-ON AMERICA SERIES

Researching, planning, and producing a book is a year's work. As I studied the rich and complex story of America's history I realized that **HANDS-ON AMERICA** is more than one book. By the time I completed an overview that scanned the past 400 years, it was evident there was a volume for each century.

VOLUME I: 1598 TO 1697 (available August, 2001)

This publication covers the **VIKINGS**, gives information on **EXPLORERS**, and concentrates on the **EASTERN WOODLAND INDIANS'** culture. The **EARLY COLONISTS'** lifestyle concludes the book.

VOLUME II: 1698 TO 1798 (available August, 2002)

The **COLONIAL ERA** is completed with 25 projects. The **SOUTHEASTERN WOODLAND INDIANS** are presented with 20 projects. **AFRICAN AMERICAN** folk art is presented with 10 projects.

VOLUME III: 1799-1900 (available August, 2003)

The **LEWIS AND CLARK EXPEDITION** is a focus with 40 projects on their scientific discoveries and the Indians they encountered from the Mississippi to the Pacific Ocean. The Spaniards' role in California, New Mexico and Texas is another **SPANISH/INDIAN** feature. The folk art of the Gold Rush, Civil War and the age of the Industrial Revolution will also be presented.

VOLUME IV: 1901-2004 (available August, 2004)

The **VICTORIAN ERA** of handcrafts will present fresh and new projects. The amazing century of Mickey Mouse and Pablo Picasso will usher in the technology and space era of today.

THE WWW.HANDS-ON.COM WEBSITE:

Books in progress will often be presented as separate activities that can be downloaded on this website. For a $4.00 charge you can download the activity page, descriptive drawings, any patterns, and often the full-color photo of the projects as they would appear in the book. There will be a place for suggestions and comments from users of these books.

Topics that are of regional interest but not for general publication will also be available on the website. This would include topics such as Antarctica, Pacific Island, Maori and Aboriginal activities that might eventually be included in a published book.

HANDS-ON ANCIENT CIVILIZATIONS will be published during the American volumes.

IMPORTANT POINTS OF INTEREST

Information on map circles: Anse aux Meadows is a Viking settlement, Christiansted was an early trading capital on St. Croix, Huronia in Ontario was home of the Huron League, Plains of Abraham in Quebec, was the site of an important battle in French and Indian War. Gay's Head on Martha's Vineyard, home to the Wampanoags and *Maushop*, a protective giant, was said to protect the people. Lake Champlain was sacred to the Western Abenaki because of *Odzihoso*, who created the world and turned himself into a rock formation on the shore of the lake. Mt. Katahadin was sacred to the Penobscot, The Falls of the Upper Delaware to the Lenape. Mystic was the site of the slaughter of the Pequot during King Philip's War.

1. L'Anse aux Meadows
2. Christiansted
3. Huronia
4. Plains of Abraham
5. Gay's Head
6. Lake Champlain
7. Niagara Falls
8. Mt. Katahadin
9. Falls of Upper Delaware
10. Oneida Lake
11. St. Augustine, Florida
12. Roanoke
13. Jamestown
14. Plymouth
15. Boston Commons
16. New Amsterdam
17. Hudson River
18. Site of King Philip's war
19. Mystic, Connecticut
20. Salem
21. Providence, Rhode Island
22. Philadelphia

MAP OF THE THIRTEEN COLONIES

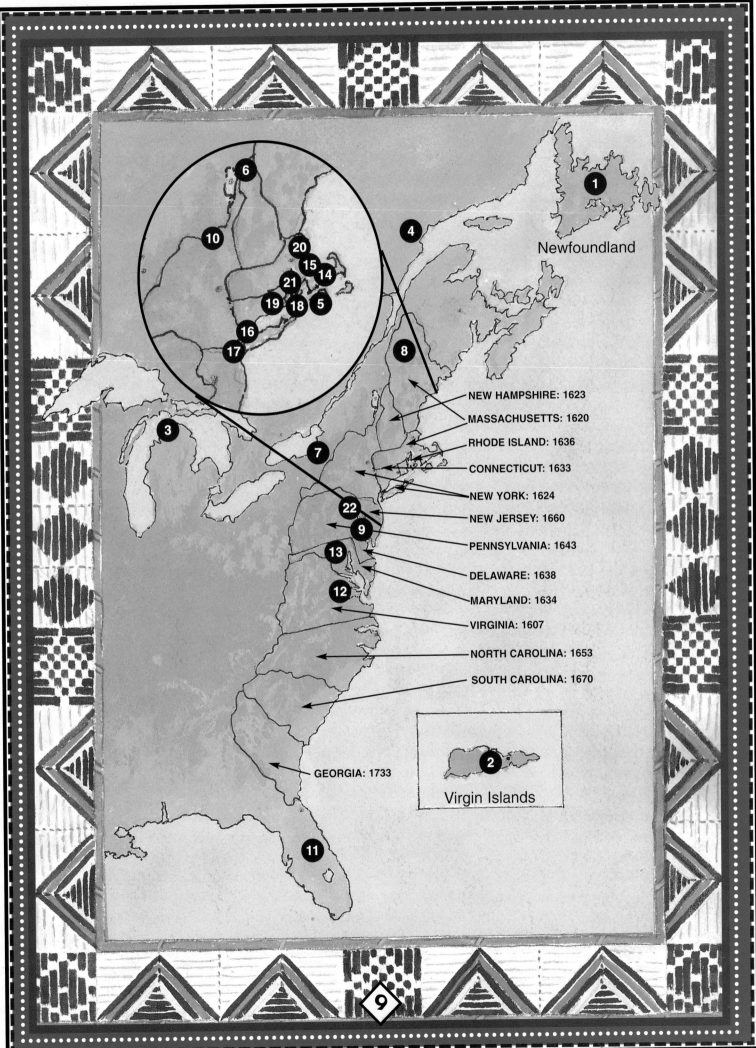

Newfoundland

NEW HAMPSHIRE: 1623

MASSACHUSETTS: 1620

RHODE ISLAND: 1636

CONNECTICUT: 1633

NEW YORK: 1624

NEW JERSEY: 1660

PENNSYLVANIA: 1643

DELAWARE: 1638

MARYLAND: 1634

VIRGINIA: 1607

NORTH CAROLINA: 1653

SOUTH CAROLINA: 1670

GEORGIA: 1733

Virgin Islands

VIKINGS AND EXPLORERS

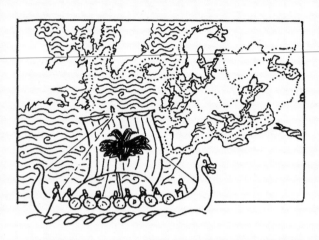

The Vikings of Sweden, Norway and Denmark explored what we now know as the British Isles, Europe, old Byzantine Empire and even Asia for 700 years. Their lust for adventure, treasure and new homes was made possible by their handsome, hand-made, easy-to-navigate boats and the discovery of the sail. The Vikings sailed west as well and built villages in Greenland. Leif Eriksson governed them but always yearned to explore further west. He left this challenge to his son Erik.

The redheaded Erik sailed west in 1000 A.D. and recorded a rocky island that is thought to be Baffin Island, then reached Labrador and finally settled in northern Newfoundland called *Anse aux Meadows* today but Vinland by the Viking navigators. The abundance of forests, grapes and game was recorded as very appealing. The remains of the longhouses, a steambath, and ironworks for 70-90 people are proof of this New World site. America may have been named from the Viking word "Omme-rike", the "remote land" in Norse.

The explorers record sailing further south to a coast where the rivers teemed with salmon, the berries and grapes grew and the game flourished. A group of canoes carrying "dark skinned men waving rattles" rowed past them. The second time a larger group of Indians stopped their canoes and exchanged gifts with the Vikings and seemed peaceable. The Vikings called the Indians "skraelings". On their third visit past the settlement the Indians waving rattles had a menacing sound and they battled the Vikings skillfully using bows and arrows and knives. The Vikings returned to Vinland convinced they could not build anything permanent on the southern coast because of the hostile natives.

the mythical Wagnerian Viking

The Vikings had a rich tradition of art as is clear from the discovery of buried furniture, magnificent carved boats, handsomely crafted jewelry and containers, beautifully woven clothing and finely made items for daily use.

A. Christopher Columbus
B. John Cabot
C. Magellan
D. Henry Hudson
E. Balboa
F. Cartier

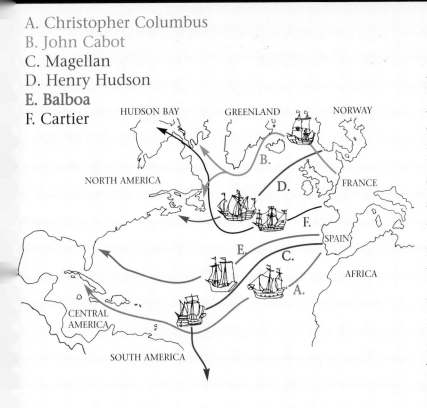

Most luxury goods were available from Asia after the Italian Marco Polo traveled to China in 1275 and stayed for 17 years. He was the first European to write an account of life in Asia. Gold, silk, spices and jewels commanded high prices for the Venetian merchants who controlled the market. Overland travel along the bandit-ridden Silk road was common but dangerous and tedious. Several European nations decided to explore another sea route to Asia. **Prince Henry the Navigator** of Portugal was an educated sailor and scientist.

Christopher Columbus was an Italian explorer whose expeditions were sponsored by the Spanish crown. Between 1492 and 1502 he made four voyages to the New World, seeking a route to Asia. He was the first European to explore the Americas and found the two best sea routes across the Atlantic Ocean.

John Cabot was an Italian hired by the English to explore the New England coast. He made two trips and claimed England's first territory in North America.

Vasco Nunez de Balboa was the first explorer to see the Pacific Ocean.

Ferdinand Magellan, a Spaniard, was the first European to sail around the world in 1519.

Jacques Cartier, a French explorer, surveyed the land that would later become Canada.

Henry Hudson, an English navigator hired by the Dutch, claimed land that was to become the first Dutch colony in North America. In 1609 he sailed the *Half Moon* up the river that would bear his name.

Samuel de Champlain was a French explorer who drew this map showing the Patuxet Indians' village in 1605. It is his view of Plymouth 15 years before the Mayflower landed. He defeated a Mohawk Iroquois raiding party with Algonquin allies in the first recorded encounter using European firearms.

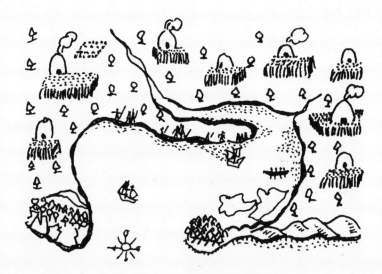

THREE VIKING HELMETS

THREE VIKING HELMETS

Easy Helmet with Paper Bag #1
Materials: Any paper bag with a width of 12", silver water-based paint or spray paint, 24" of silver duct tape, stapler, newspaper, pencil, scissors, and visor. Pattern on page 86.

Fold a piece of newspaper in half with 6" on each side of fold. Copy the helmet pattern on page 86. Pencil the lines on half of the fold. Cut out the newspaper visor, eyeholes and sloping front of helmet. Now trace it onto the paper bag. Cut out the visor on the front half of the helmet. Cut the sides of the helmet (leaving the 3" folded sides untouched) so it slopes to a peak at the top. Staple the sides, paint the paper bag with silver paint, or spray paint the bag on both sides. When the bag is dry add the duct tape strips:
a. tape a 1" strip around the base of the helmet
b. tape a 1" strip down the front from the top to the nosepiece
c. tape duct tape eyebrows on the visor
d. tape 1/2" strips to resemble metal seams

Helmet with Nose Guard #2
Materials: Triangle pattern, manila folder, silver wrapping paper, glue, stapler, scissors, pencil.

Using the triangle pattern cut 4 cardboard shapes and 4 silver shapes. Glue the silver to the cardboard. Notch the edges every inch from the base to the top. Cut paper and cardboard strips (1)1"x 24" and (2) 1"x 18". Glue silver paper to cardboard. Staple the silver edges of the triangle pieces to each other. Punch out the curved sides when you are finished. Try on your helmet for size. Staple the silver strip around the helmet base, the longest strip in front extending 4 inches as a nose guard. Staple the side strip.

The third helmet #3 is continued on page 77.

First and foremost, Viking men were warriors. Their welding skill with various metals created helmets and swords of pride and individuality. When a group of Viking longboats landed on a foreign beach, the fierce Vikings were in the enemy stronghold in minutes with their minimal armor and weaponry. They marauded monasteries most frequently because that is where the Church kept its treasures and defenses were weak. Excavated Viking helmets have carved snakes over the top seam, lions for brows, and etched figures of gods and goddesses in the metals. A Viking was buried with his war gear, his furniture and sometimes even his long boat.

VIKING JEWELRY

VIKING JEWELRY

The Round Brooch for Fastening Shawls and Tunic Straps
Materials: Aluminum cooking sheet, circle shape, nail or toothpick for etching, skewer, silver paint, silver cardboard, hole punch.

There are several brooch styles in the photograph. The three-sided "trefoil" was the most popular. Cut out the shape from the foil. Carefully mark the design with a sharp point. Punch two holes and stick a silver painted skewer through the holes to catch your shawl and hold it in place.

The Hammer of Thor Pendant
Materials: Aluminum foil, sharp point, silver marker, lacing.

Thor was the son of the god, Odin. He was much admired for his strength in combatting evil. He used his mighty hammer for good and it was a good luck omen. Study the hammer's shape. One has a top of an animal head. All have used "repousee" or etching into a metal surface for the design. Remember to plan how you will fasten your string.

Necklaces
Materials: Salt dough clay recipe on page 19. Silver paper and silver wrapping paper rolled into beads, scissors, glue, strong string, pink, blue, green, yellow paint, brush, toothpicks.

Ordinary Viking women wore necklaces of brightly colored glass beads of these same colors. A small silver bead might separate them. Wealthier women wore silver beads with silver coins as separators. Make your salt dough. Roll the beads and stick them on a toothpick. Loosen the bead for easy removal. Let beads dry and then paint them. Now remove from toothpick and string with rolled silver paper separators.

The Gotland Stone
Materials: Plaster of Paris in a round mold, 2 straws to make the holes, a nail point for etching, carefully applied black and brown paint, twine.

When your circle of plaster has dried, scratch your design into it. Clean off the powder. Gently finger rub paint over your plaster. Put twine through the holes.

Viking men and women prided themselves on their appearance. Their handwoven clothes were linen and wool, dyed with bright colors. The wealthy wore silk as raiders discovered the East. The Viking raider often buried his treasure and then never returned to it. Jewelry taken from the Byzantine countries, Franks, Anglo-Saxons and Scandinavians was worn with pride.

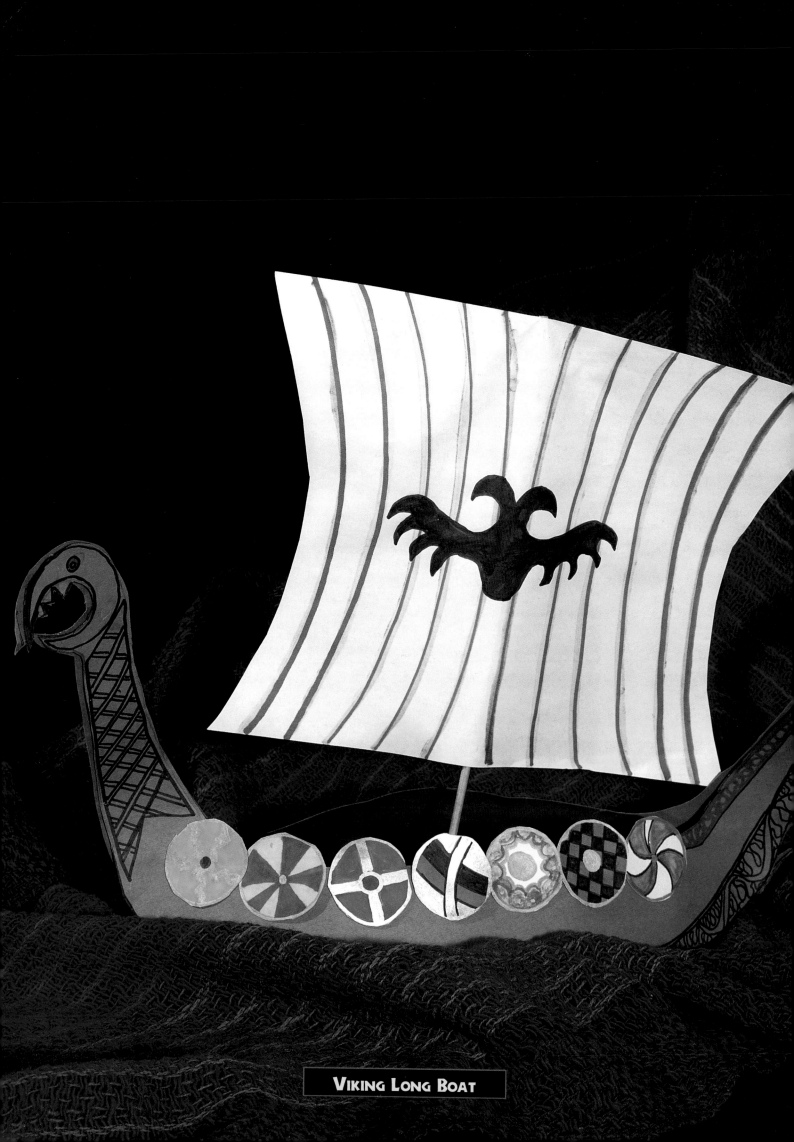

VIKING LONG BOAT

THE VIKING LONG BOAT

Materials: Four pieces of brown paper 12" x 18", glue, scissors, two enlarged patterns on page 87, black and colored fine-tipped markers, a gold and silver marker is nice but optional, a 1" circle shape, 8" x 11" white paper for sail, wooden skewer. Design ideas are on page 74.

Enlarge the pattern for the side of the ship, making 2 copies. Enlarge the pattern for the bottom making 1 copy. Glue two pieces of the brown paper together so you have two double-strength pieces. Trace the patterns on the paper and cut them out. Reglue all edges, especially the boat bottom piece. After studying Viking scrollwork and the rune alphabet make designs on the sides of the boat as in the photograph. Highlight the bird head and the fern scroll prows. Notch the bottom of the boat about 1/4" and 1/2" apart on both sides **all along each side**.

Put glue on the wrong side of the boat bottom and stick it to the bottom of the boat side. Press each paper part together until they are bonded. Do this to the second side as well. You have now built a fine boat bottom, almost exactly as the Vikings did. You can make the colorful shields and glue them to the sides of the boat, waiting for battle. We know the Vikings had sails. Cut your sail from a piece of white paper. Round two sides. Make any design on your sail you wish creating your own image.

Glue a skewer to the middle back of the sail. This wooden pole is called the "mainstay" and was very important for navigation. To secure the sail and mainstay cut two pieces of brown paper 3 1/2" square. Glue them to the boat center. Cut four strips 1/4" x 5" long and fold them in half. Glue the doubled strips now 1/4" x 2 1/2" to each side of the skewer and down into the reinforced boat bottom.

The Vikings loved their long boats. Some were 70 to 100 feet long. The sail gave them swiftness as most other ships were moved by rowing. They had a rudder so they were easily maneuvered. Each ship had a name, often pictured on the huge sail, such as Long Serpent or Bison The prows were often carved dragon heads, fierce birds or natural coils. When they were in the harbor, their shields rested on the ship sides. Each sailor had a trunk of personal things. He sat on the trunk to row the ship. Vikings usually stayed near the coast and camped on the beaches.

A VIKING GAME

A VIKING GAME

Materials: Salt dough recipe**(15 birds for one-third recipe), cloth square
15" x 15", brown, yellow, white water-base paint, brush, water, markers, a dime.

Making the Birds
Take a wad of salt dough clay the size of a grape.
Have a container of water ready. Roll the dough until
it is round and smooth. Use the water to create smooth
lines. Carefully form the tail and the head of the bird.
Smooth the bottom to be the size of a dime. Put the bird
on a dime and make sure it measures that size. Air dry
the birds overnight or bake them in a 200 degree
oven for several hours. You should use 10 to 15 birds
for a game.

Painting the Birds
Brush a color onto the bird from your paint palette.
Brush a contrasting color on in a few dabs. Either rub
with your fingers or use the brush to blend the colors.
Only blend a little or the birds will not look aged.
Let the paint dry.

Playing the Game
Cup all the birds in your hand. Your cloth is laid out on
a surface. Throw the birds onto the cloth. You get a point
for any bird that lands upright. You get two points for any
bird that lands in a circle and three points for a bird that lands
upright and on a circle.

Vikings spent long, boring hours in their long boats
or in their winter longhouses. Simple gambling games
were an amusement. The birds were carved of ivory,
stone or wood. They were carried in a pouch with
the game cloth. Some games have been found in
excavated burial sites. The Greenland Eskimos played
a similar game.

**Recipe for stiff salt dough: 1 cup salt, 2 cups flour, 4 teaspoons cream of tartar, 2 cups cold
water. Mix all **dry** ingredients in a cooking pot. Add water and cook over medium heat,
stirring, until dough forms a ball.

ODIN'S RAVEN

ODIN'S RAVEN

Easy Small Raven
Materials: Construction paper, 11"x 13", scissors, pattern on page 88, glue, crayon or oil pastels, drawing paper.

Enlarge and copy the raven pattern on page 88 and cut it out. Trace the cutout onto a fold of the black paper. Cut out the central oval. Cut out the bird with two heads. Trace the oval onto a piece of drawing paper. Have the students draw their impression of the Viking God Odin. Cut out the drawing leaving 1/2" edge for gluing. Glue to the back of the raven and add the eyes and feet.

Flapping Winged Raven
Materials: Black poster board 24" x 15", black paper scraps, scissors, dark brown, light brown, red paper, glue, bird head pattern.

1. Enlarge this bird pattern to measure a rectangle 24"x 15". Fold the triangle in half. Cut the headless body of the raven. Cut out a central oval that is 6"x 8" for Odin's face.
2. Cut the wings 1/2" from each side of the oval.
3. Cut out the raven head from the pattern, to be assembled later.
4. Using drawing paper trace Odin's oval and begin the paper sculpture or draw your version of Odin's face with as much texture as possible: fur for hair, etc. Glue your Odin face in place.
5. Make black feather details to enhance the wings. Glue a taped hinge on the top and bottom of each wing. Color the tape black. Glue the black feather designs over the tape.
6. Assemble the raven head and glue on top of neck. Add a bright necklace to hide the seams. Add eyes and feet.

Odin was the chief god of the Vikings. He had only one eye as he had exchanged the other for wisdom. He is usually depicted with his two ravens Hugimum and Munimum who perched on his shoulder and whispered secrets and news into his ears.

THE WOODLAND INDIAN CULTURE

 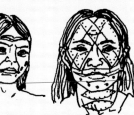

The so-called "Woodland" cultural area has been assigned to all tribes living east of the Mississippi River between the Gulf of Mexico and James Bay. Our focus is on the most important area in the early development of the United States and the tribes in the region who played a significant role in shaping the New World's history. It has been suggested that French may have been the national language had not Iroquois hatred of the French been greater than their distrust of the English. There is evidence that the American constitution was influenced by the philosophy of the Iroquois League.

APPEARANCE

Early descriptions show admiration for the physical appearance of the Natives. They were tall, straight, muscular and well proportioned. Obesity and deformities were rare. They had high, prominent cheekbones, widely separated eyes and their skin was a light bronzed color, smooth and clear. Facial painting was common with both men and women with red the most popular color used. Red was also rubbed on body parts and on possessions. Most of the red paint was from central Maine. This love of staining the body red was why early settlers called them "red men." Bear grease protected them from insects and cold. Often the body was "smoked" with sage and sweet herbs. Tattooing was common, especially on the cheeks. Baldness was rare. **Men and women both** wore breech clouts of soft animal skin about 48 inches long and suspended from a belt with flaps hanging down in front and back.

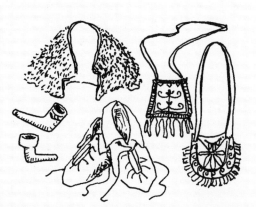

Shoulder capes called mantles were fastened over the left shoulder. They were held in place by a belt, often hollow for storing dried food. Mantles might be woven grass, fine white moose skin with a red, blue or yellow border, or woven feathers. The favored cold weather cape was of raccoon as the draping tails were impressive. The best moccasins were made from moose hide. The sole was a separate piece. Flaps were raised for warmth or protection. When the moccasins began to wear the wearer switched them to the other foot. Quill, hemp, beads and cloth decorated the toe and flaps.

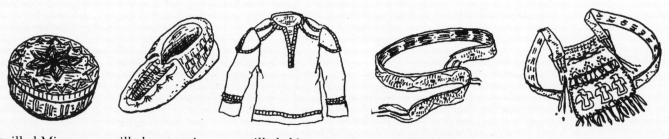

quilled Micmac box   quilled moccasins   quilled skin coat   quilled belts   quilled pouch

Before the Historic period women mostly wore the breechclout. By the time of the colonists they were wearing a type of skirt. Women wore red paint on their foreheads, temples and cheeks and young women wore black dye around their eyes. Their mantles were longer and larger and dragged on the ground.

Occasionally a shorter mantle, a sort of a jacket, was worn as an upper covering. Skin tubes covered the lower leg with a garter holding them in place. Combs, necklaces and decorative beadwork adorned women and their clothing. The tedious but handsome skill of **Quilling** was applied to bark, skin clothing and other surfaces in subtly dyed patterns. The quill worker softened the dyed quill in the mouth or water and flattened it with the teeth or fingernail, biting off the dark brown tip. Applying the quill to bark involved punching holes but no sewing.

WOOD AND BARK were the most important materials to the forest Indians. Bark was a cradle-to-grave material: the cradle board for every baby with a bark funnel going from the carrier to dispose of baby waste, containers for every need, raingear capes and conical hats, wigwam homes, canoes, a burial shroud for bodies which were placed in fetal position and then painted red and wrapped in birch bark before burial.

Domed and conical wigwams were known throughout the northern forests. The Iroquois used longhouses for several families with wooden frames and overlaid bark roofs and sides. Birch bark sap dishes, funnel-shaped containers, and folded bark trays and buckets could be made in an hour. A double bucket could hold 2-3 gallons of water. The "**crooked knife**" was introduced by white traders, but the Indians refined it as a nearly "all-purpose" utensil. It was named for the upturned blade. It was speedy and efficient in carving snowshoe frames, toboggans, bows, arrows, paddles, clubs, and splint baskets. European traders adopted the Indian objects, especially the indispensable canoe and snowshoe.

STONE BOWLS were replaced with **clay pots** after the Huron from Ohio region introduced pottery in 500 B.C. The stone bowls had been made by men. The pottery industry was completely the women's domain as were the planting, harvesting and storage of grown foods. The first pots were pointed at the bottom and sat in the fire. As the pots evolved with more and more decorative reliefs, they became the crenelated collar pots unique to this culture. The flat-bottomed pots showed the influence of colonist's iron containers. The wide bottom distributed heat more quickly and evenly.

an early pointed bottom pot   decorated   collared/decorated pots   beginning of neck   the wide-bottom pot

THE GARDEN was the focus of women and was a source of great pride and industry. With handmade hoes they grew the "three sisters" beans, corn and squash, as well as Jerusalem artichokes, sunflowers, gourds and tobacco.

THE FOUNDING INDIAN FATHERS

seal of league

When Europeans arrived in America there were already civilizations as ancient as the Greek or Egyptian. The Indian cultures surprised the Europeans because they weren't all alike. Some, but not all, were ruled by powerful people and some were a democratic league. In some tribes women had political powers and status and some practiced slavery.

THE IROQUOIS CONFEDERATION was organized by Hiawatha and Deganwidah sometime between 1000 and 1450. They developed a constitution called The Great Law of Peace. It united Mohawk, Onondaga, Seneca, Oneida and Cayuga. Each tribe elected representatives called *sachems* that met as a council at least one year in five at a special council building. They had powers to "declare war and make peace, send and receive emissaries, enter into treaties of alliance, regulate the

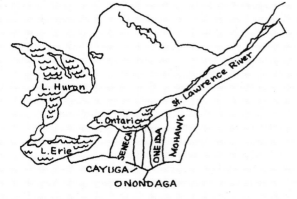

map of Iroquois League affairs of conquered nations, receive new members, and extend protection over feeble tribes." In a word, they were to promote their prosperity and enlarge their dominion.

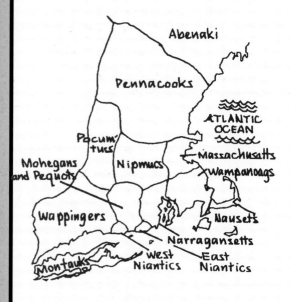

New World writers were amazed at the Indians' personal liberties, particularly their freedom from rules and social classes which is likely because there was no individual property ownership. A Huron in 1683 explained, "We are born free and united as brothers, each as much a great lord as the tribal other while you are all slaves of one man (the king). I am subject only to counsel of the Great Spirit." The modern nations of democracy based on egalitarian principles and a federated government of overlapping powers arose from a unique blend of European and Indian political ideas along the Atlantic coast from 1607 to 1776.

The nations of the Iroquois controlled territory from New England to the Mississippi River, and they built a league that endured for centuries. Unlike European governments the league blended the sovereignty of several nations into one government. This was precisely the solution to the same problem which confronted the writers of the U.S. Constitution. Today we call this a "federal" system. In fact, the Indians invented it even though the United States patented it. A Dakota Indian named Luther Standing Bear wrote:

"While the white people had much to teach us, we had much to teach them, and what a school could have been established upon that ideal... Only the white man saw nature as a 'wilderness,' and only to him was the land 'infested' with 'wild animals and savage people'. To us it was tame. Earth was bountiful and we were surrounded with the blessings of the Great Mystery."

Narraganset Chief

Important Indian Leaders of the Seventeenth Century

MASSASOIT was *sachem* of the Wampanoags from 1590 to 1661. He lived near Rhode Island. The peace treaty he signed in 1621 with the Pilgrims was never broken. It was Massasoit and his 90 Indians who joined the newcomers for the First Thanksgiving. Massasoit, Squanto and other helpful Indians can take much of the credit for the survival of the early colonists. They taught them much about farming, hunting and how to catch, prepare, and eat the seafood.

WAMSUTTA and METACOM were the sons of Massasoit. They were given the English names of Philip and Alexander, after the great Greek heroes. They were unhappy that such a large number of settlers had come while their people and father had kept peace with the landgrabbing Europeans. When Wamsutta (Alexander) was kidnapped and died a mysterious death, Metacom (Philip) waged a devastating and brutal war called King Philip's War: 1675-76. Three thousand Indians died and six hundred colonists lost their lives.

LAPPAWINSOE was a Delaware Indian chief who signed an agreement with Pennsylvania colonists giving them all the land they could cover on foot in one and a half days. The colonists chose their fastest runners and doubled the amount Lappawinsoe expected. He felt cheated by the too-clever Europeans.

CANONINCUS (kuh NON in kuss) was the Narraganset chief Roger Williams bought Providence Rhode Island from in 1636. The treaty between the two remarkable men lasted the 40 years known as The Golden Age. The Indian chief, Miantonomo, also signed.

POWHATAN was the father of Pocahontas and one of the wealthiest men in the New World. He had 2-12 wives; lesser chiefs paid him tribute. He had great wealth in skins, beads, copper, pearls, deer, turkeys, wild beasts and corn. When he travelled he had 40-50 bodyguards, the tallest men his nation could provide.

CANASSATEGO, an Iroquois chief who spoke at an Indian-British assembly in Pennsylvania in 1744, complained that the Indians found it difficult to deal with so many different colonial administrations each with its own policy. Couldn't the colonists form a Union and speak with one voice? He recommended not only what they should do but also *how they should do it*. He encouraged them to study the Iroquois League which had already accomplished this several hundred years earlier.

THREE INDIAN HAIRSTYLES

THREE INDIAN HAIRSTYLES

Materials: Four ounces of black yarn, 2 yards of black "school" paper, 1 black railroad board, scissors, brown paper, stapler, glue, fine-tipped markers, oil pastels, yarn, small real feathers, fake paper feathers, paper cutter, 1/4" graph paper.

Basic HeadPiece

1. Cut a band of black railroad board 1 1/2" x 24" long. Measure it around the wearer's head. Staple the ends to fit.
2. Cut a second strip 1 1/2" x 14". Staple it to the exact front of the first headband, measure it across the wearer's head, and staple it securely to the back center headband. **(*Do not staple this piece for the braid hairstyle. Set it aside.)**

Porcupine Roach Hairstyle (stands upright down the top of the head)

1. Measure 5-6 layers of black paper 18" x 5" . Cut through all paper layers and make the roach shape of 3" front tapering to 5" to the end. Cut the five inches tapering 2" in from the front so most of the roach is 5" high (see drawing).
2. Cut thin fringe on the paper cutter *being careful to leave 1 1/2" uncut at the roach base. It should look like hair.*
3. Cut two black railroad board strips 3" x 18" long. Score each 1" in from the edge and fold it. Staple strip to the base of the fringed roach. Cutting for curving, staple it to the overband. Insert a few inches of new fringe and glue wherever you have gaps.
4. Decorate graph paper and create a handsome beaded band and glue it around your roach hairstyle. Make fake eagle feathers and glue into the roach.

(B)

(A)

Classic Braids

1. Wrap yarn in 10-foot loops. You will need two to four ounces of black yarn. Hold yarn in half and cut each five foot end. You should have 100 strands of five foot yarn strands.
2. Lay them over the (A) cut band to go over the head with 2 1/2 feet on each side of the band. Staple and glue in place. Glue a second black paper band (B) over the middle band to hide the gluing and stapling. Braid each side. It is easiest to braid if someone is wearing the band like real braiding.
3. Make a lovely colorful beaded design with markers and place it over the braids.

Activity is continued on page 78.

CORN HUSK MASKS

Corn Husk Masks

The Authentic Corn Husk Mask
Materials: Two paper plates 10–11" round, prepared painted white school paper 24" x 24" cut in 1/4" to 1/2" strips, yellow, ochre and brown paint, big brush, a two-ounce bunch of natural raffia, scissors, glue, stapler, big-eyed needle and string or thread.

1. Tie your raffia bundles by looping five strands of raffia into a 6" bunch. Tie off one end and cut the loops of the untied end. Make 20 to 25 of these. Staple and glue them to the rim of the inverted bottom paper plate, fluffing the raffia to create a fullness.

2. Create the corn husk colored woven face using a big brush to apply yellow, ochre and brown paint to a piece of white school paper. Cut in 1/4" to 1/2" strips after it has dried.

3. Weave the strips together so they cover the top paper plate. Lay on the plate, turning the paper fringe under the rim and stapling in place. Make a 24" long piece of braided raffia and glue around the edge to cover any sloppiness.

4. Cut a nose of scrap painted paper or weave 1/8" strands into a nose. Glue into the middle of the face.

5. Put the top plate on top of the bottom plate. Thread a big-eyed needle with yellow yarn, thread or string. With 2" stitches attach the two plates together around the edge. With a scissors tip or Exacto knife carefully cut through the small eyes and mouth. They are quite small in the authentic masks.

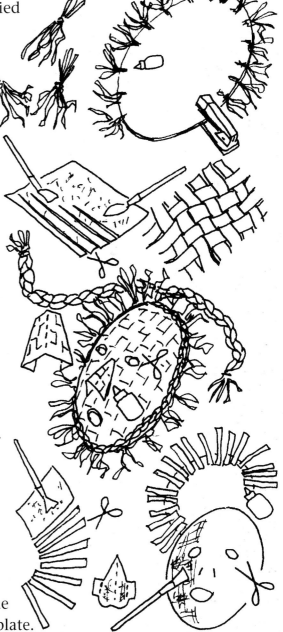

Simple Paper Plate Mask
Materials: Two plain paper plates 8", an 8 1/2 x 11" piece of paper painted with a big brush and yellow, brown and ochre paint, small brush, stapler, glue, 18" of braided raffia, yarn or twine for mask trim around the edge.

1. Paint the paper, let it dry and cut strips 1/2" to 4" wide and long. Staple or glue around the edge of the bottom plate.

2. Paint the top paper plate with the same paint to look woven. Use a small brush. Cut out a painted nose with slots and insert into the middle of the face. Glue and staple the top plate on top of the bottom plate. Cut out the small eyes and mouth to fit the wearer's face.

Most masks were burned after the harvest ceremony. We know of their existence from artists' drawings and descriptions.

DELAWARE TURKEY RATTLE

DELAWARE TURKEY RATTLE

Materials: Two cardboard pieces 5"x7", brown, green, yellow oil pastels, beans or unpopped corn for rattle, green felt, 1/2" dowel 10" long, feathers, a green felt square, colored paper or felt strips, glue, scissors, nail, several paper clips.

1. Look carefully at the crafted turtle rattle and the authentic turtle rattle. The shell design is beautiful. The color can be interpreted as green, black or brown. See pattern on page 92.

2. Cut the two pieces of cardboard to match the pattern. Color the top shell first with yellow oil pastels, then color with brown and finally a dark green. Rub the crayons together with a fingertip. On a separate piece of paper pencil the shell design. Using a nail end scratch the design into the crayon. Go over it with the tip of the yellow oil pastel. The bottom design is yellow with typical turtle patterns that look like this. Include the bottom head in one piece. Finally make the top headpiece. Snip 1/2" cuts 1" apart around top and bottom shells.

3. Put the rattle beans in between the two shells and stick 1 1/2" of the stick into the turtle, gluing both sides of the shell all around. (You can get more height for the shell by stuffing tissue between the shells, but you might give up the full rattle.) Compress the glue with several paper clips. Insert the heads to plug up that end and glue all three cardboards together: head and two shells. Secure with paper clips.

4. Cut three felt strips, 1" x 10" long. Wind the first around the glue-covered dowel. Overlap the second and third strip to go under the turtle shell on both sides, insuring that there are no gaps for the rattles to drop out. Add feathers, stuck under a ribbon or felt strip and add the colorful paper or felt strips.

Many groups made turtle shell rattles as a part of the healing ceremonies. The Lenape (Delaware) wore a bearskin, and a two-sided face mask and carried a crooked stick. The wearer is impersonating *Mesingw, Keeper of the Game,* who controlled the forest creatures.

TWO POUCHES

TWO POUCHES

Iroquois Thunderbird Pouch

Materials: 9" square of black and brown paper, plus a 20" x 1 1/2" strip of brown paper, 2" x 9" and 1/4" squares and 20" strip of graph paper, 12" of several colorful ribbons or yarn or thin paper strips, glue, scissors, fine-tipped markers, 30 colorful beads with BIG holes, oil pastel crayons, one yard of yarn for fringe, pencil, ruler, big-eyed needle.

1. Cut the black paper square and brown backing square to slightly angle at the top. Using a pencil and the pattern ideas on page 74 design the three strips of the pouch on the graph paper and the handle "beaded" design.

2. Use oil pastel crayons and cover the pencil design with the vivid colors on the bottom band. Next make the "faux beaded" top bag band and the strap. This is time-consuming art but the results are beautiful.

3. Using a long piece of yarn, thread the big-eyed needle and string two beads, then cut to be 2" long. Leave enough yarn at top for gluing. Make 25-30 beaded fringes.

4. Assembling the bag parts. Look at the black bag front and add any borders or designs it might need. Make a glue line around the edges and bottom of the bag. Lay the beaded fringe parts in place. Lay the black bag front on the brown backing so they are glued together.

5. Glue the gridded strap to the brown paper strip. The brown should show about 1/4" on both edges. Put a glue line where strap will be attached to the bag and lay cut ribbons in place. Glue strap in place with ribbons secured. Place a heavy book on glued bag for an hour while the glue sets and dries.

The Paper Bag with a Pipe Design (The smaller bag with the pipe design is the same process, though it is all made of paper.)

Pouches hung from the belts of men and women. They held flint, steel and tinder for fire-making, or tobacco and a clay pipe. Often the pouch was the whole fur body of a small rodent such as a squirrel, otter, mink, weasel or muskrat. The legs and tail were left on the body. This pouch was often worn around the neck.

MEN'S LEATHER LEGGINGS

MEN'S LEATHER LEGGINGS

Materials: Two 12" x 24" inch prepared animal skin-looking paper, see page 77, grid paper 18" x 8", 5 dark brown paper strips 20" x 8", fine-tipped markers, ruler, scissors, pencil, glue, stapler. For a durable costume use tan colored cloth and commercial braid.

1. Measure the legs to wear the leggings from waist to top of the foot. Cut two sets of leggings about 12" wide and 24" long. Fold in half and glue or staple together. Cut double 1"fringe. **Make sure the fringe is on the outside of the leggings.**

2. Measure two grid papers 1 1/2" x 20" to decorate the sides of the leggings. Look at page 74 for authentic Indian designs.

3. Measure two 1" x 18" grid papers for the mid-leg gaiter ties. Decorate with markers in faux beaded designs.

4. Measure the band for the waist after measuring the wearer's waist. Cut a grid paper 2" x 20" depending on the measurement. Decorate it with markers.

5. Cut brown paper strips for mounting the decorative bands. Glue the legging strips onto the fringe side of the leggings. Tie the midleg band and attach the leggings to the waistband by tying onto the band.

These deerskin tubes were worn by men. Women's were shorter and lower. They were warm and practical as they gave protection from the brush and brambles along the trail. They were held in place by thongs that tied them to the waist. They were often painted with decoration. They tied under the foot where a moccasin covered the leather stirrup.

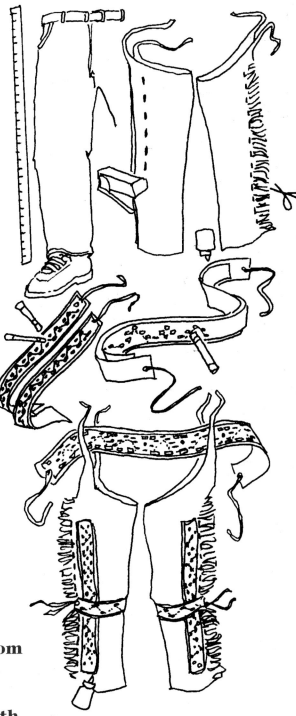

HANDSOME COLLARED POTS

HANDSOME COLLARED POTS

Materials: Salt dough recipe on page 19, a small round container like a butter tub, plastic fork, plastic knife, pencil, ruler or other "paddle" for smoothing coils.

1. Make a lump of clay the size of an orange. Divide it almost in half. With the smaller "half" form a base inside the round container or use your hands. Roll several finger-thick coils. Join them into circles the size of your base. Press coils onto base and attach them by smoothing inside and outside. Repeat until your pot is the desired height.

2. If you are making an early woodland pot (pointed end) as shown in our photograph, add coils until the pot is 5" high. Make the pointed bottom by rolling the end until it is rounded and pointed.

3. If you are making the later woodland pot with the flat bottom add more coils until the pot is 6" to 7" high. Press your pencil 1 1/2" from the top and press all around the pot to form a neck.

4. Using the plastic knife, cut 1/2" away from the rim leaving two points. Smooth the sides of both pots using a ruler, a butter knife or paddle. Keep the fingers of one hand inside for support, carefully patting the sides smooth.

5. Finish the pot by decorating with plastic fork tines. Early pottery was simply decorated but later had these designs:

Migrating Adena Indians brought clay pots from the Ohio Valley in 500 B.C. They were molded to a point so they would sit upright in the hearth and the fire was built up the sides. Eventually the bottom became flat and the collar allowed for the pot to hang above the fire and have even heat distribution. By 1600 these were typical Indian pots in the northern colonial region. The decorated collar is a departure from most early Indian pot traditions.

BIRCH BARK CANOE

BIRCH BARK CANOE

Materials: A rectangle of birch-bark-prepared manila cardboard 6" x 12", bark looking paper on page 77, four cut bark strips 1/2" x 12", 1 yard of yellow-orange yarn, big-eyed needle, paper clips, scissors, two toothpicks, hammer, nail and pounding surface.

1. Fold the bark-prepared cardboard in half so it measures 3" x 12". Round the ends with scissors.

2. Cut a small notch in the four strips about every 2". The notch should be 1/8". **Do not notch close to the strip top edge.**

3. Using a newspaper pile as a cushioned surface, pound two nail holes close together every 1 1/2" along the canoe's two rims and down the curved ends.

4. Glue each narrow strip and sew onto the top of the canoe rim, using the notches to ease the strip with the curve of the canoe. Glue and secure the strips with paper clips until dry. The gluing step can be skipped and the two strips can be sewn, making the notched strips curve with the canoe.

5. Sew the ends. Study the photograph to see how the sewing looks.

6. Pull the sides of the canoe apart and insert the two toothpicks 3" apart.

The stands of paper birch in New Hampshire and Maine were rightly known as "canoe birch". Bark from these giants (some were 30" in diameter) yielded the best bark during a winter thaw. The European trappers and New World colonizers were amazed with the birch bark canoe of the northern Indian. Swift on the water, it could be easily managed by a single paddler. It could hold great loads yet it was light enough for one man to carry. The Iroquois boasted of a canoe that carried 50 men over the Great Lakes. Raw materials were everywhere for repair. The craft was sturdy and waterproof and, when weighted with stones and sunk, the canoe would be ready for use after months of submersion.

IROQUOIS FALSE FACE MASKS

IROQUOIS FALSE FACE MASKS

Blue Mask with Painted Paper Hair #1
Materials: A paper plate, red and blue paint, brush, scissors, pencil, blue marker, 6" square of white paper, hair of raffia or yarn, stapler. Patterns are on page 90.
1. Copy and cut out the mouth and nose shapes on page 90.
Cut white round paper eyes. Paint the paper plate and
the cut nose blue. Notch the nose in place.
Glue on the eyes.
2. Paint the mouth shape red and make a hole in
the center. Make four 1" cuts on both sides of the
plate. Staple the cuts so they create a curved face.
Glue the red mouth in place, making a hole in the
plate. Staple or glue hair in place.

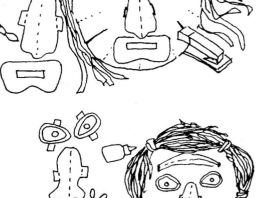

Crooked Face Mask with Raffia Hair #2
Materials: 12" x 12" manila cardboard or railroad board prepared to resemble bark (see page 77), red and white paper, 1 yard of natural or black raffia, glue, scissors, pencil.
1. Prepare the cardboard to look like wood. Using the
patterns cut out the nose and red mouth. Cutting the
notch places on the face, notch them onto the face
(the face is so crooked it can't be wrong). Glue on the eyes.
2. Wrap the raffia in four places 6" apart so it is easier
to glue. Glue it onto the face. Cut a hole in the mouth.

Brown Paper Big-Nose Mask with Black Yarn #3
Materials: 12" x 9" of brown paper, brown and red markers, white paper, 10 yards of black yarn, scissors, pencil.
1. Cut the pointed head shape from the brown paper. Cut nose pattern on
darker piece of paper or use the brown marker to color it. Notch nose
onto face. Cut out the crooked mouth on face and outline with red.
Cut out eyes and glue on face. Bunch black yarn and glue in place.

**The False Face or Medicine Mask has the recognizable distorted
nose and mouth. The mouth always has a hole as the healer
blew healing air through it onto the sick person. The myth
is that a giant challenged the Creator to move a mountain. The
giant only nudged the shape but the Creator moved it in seconds. The giant
turned in amazement and smashed his nose crooked on the up-close mountain
peak. The masks were carved directly on the tree and then cut away to complete
the details.**

PASSAMAQUODDY BIRCH BARK ART

PASSAMAQUODDY BIRCH BARK ART

Materials: *A birch-bark prepared cardboard piece 20" x 24", glue, scissors, nail, pencil, paper and ruler. See technique page 77.*

Birch Bark Picture Frame

1. Cut out the prepared cardboard.
2. Using a ruler mark the frame division lines lightly with a pencil. Next carefully incise them with a nail point into the layered crayon. The incision line should be light colored.
3. Using a pencil and paper draw important symbols that are to appear on the frame. Think about birds, trees, plants and flowers. Think about animals that might be pets. Copy your best practice drawings onto the frame boxes, lightly penciling in the shapes. Incise the pencil lines with a nail point.
4. Cut out the frame hole the size it should be for the picture you are to frame. A paper matte for the picture is optional but looks nice. Glue the matte and picture to the back of the frame.

Round Lidded Box

1. Make 2 circle shapes on the prepared cardboard with a lid. Cut a cardboard strip 4" by the circumference of the circles.
2. Score 1/2" smaller circle on each and cut notches 1" apart to the circle line.
3. Using the nail point, scratch designs into the surfaces of the band and the circle chosen to be the lid.
4. Glue the band ends. Make a strip of glue on the inside edge of the band bottom. Fold the notches of the box bottom and insert in the bottom, with the notches catching the glue.
5. Fold the notches of the lid and glue them together, holding in place with a rubber band. They should fit inside the box band.

Activity is continued on page 78.

INDIAN JEWELRY

INDIAN JEWELRY

Penobscot Embroidered Collar
Materials: 12"x 9" black and tan paper, oil pastels, 36 inches of yarn, scissors, pencil, glue, ruler, hole punch, pattern on page 89.

1. Cut the collar shape following the screened pattern on this page. Look at page 74 for design ideas. The collar decorations were symmetrical. Fold the paper in half and quarters or divide with a ruler into four penciled sections.

2. Using a pencil lightly sketch the design onto the black paper. Next color it with oil pastels. Glue the collar to the tan paper, punch hole at each end and string knotted-ends of the yarn ties.

Bone or Antler Combs
Materials: See comb patterns on page 87, Exacto knife, pencil, ruler, scissors, antler-looking cardboard, see technique on page 77.

1. Using the comb patterns or an original comb idea draw the pattern onto the antler-prepared cardboard.

2. Have a thick pile of newspapers to protect the surface if you cut with an exacto knife. Work slowly and carefully with adult supervision.

Silver Gorget
Materials: An aluminum baking sheet, pencil, scissors, hole punch, and colorful tie.

1. Pattern for gorget is on page 89. Cut it out and draw outline on the baking sheet with a pencil. Make a pencil groove 1/4" inside the edge.

2. Punch a hole on each end and insert knotted end of tie.

Porcupine Quilled Earrings
Materials: 10 pointed-end toothpicks, whiteout, black marker, colorful felt, scissors, glue, pattern page 89.

1. Cut two pieces of felt in the earring shape.

2. Paint toothpicks 3/4 white with black marker ends.

3. Glue to the felt band. Glue another piece of contrasting felt over the toothpick tops.

The silver gorget was usually the gift of a European military commander to a chief or warrior for excellent service. They were sometimes round and often several were worn at once.

THREE MUSICAL INSTRUMENTS

THREE MUSICAL INSTRUMENTS

The Dew Claw Ankle Rattle

Materials: Paint-treated paper 10" x 20" on page 77, scissors, glue, paper clips, scrunchy, big-eyed needle, thread. Pattern on page 91.

1. Cut 20 shapes using the pattern on page 91. Roll each piece into a cone. Glue the edge and stick a paper clip up the edge while glue dries.

2. Make a hole at each cone tip with a big-eyed needle. Thread the needle and sew each cone to the scrunchy about 1/2" apart. When the scrunchy is worn on the wrist or ankle it should resemble the dew claw rattle.

The Birch Bark Rattle

Materials: Birch-bark-prepared cardboard (page 77), 1/4" x 6-8" felt strips or yarn, 12 big-holed beads, oil pastels, glue, scissors.

1. Cut the prepared cardboard in the shape on page 91. Color a design on the front from the design ideas on page 74.

2. Glue the bottom and sides together. String the beads to the strips. Glue to the top. Put some beans, corn or rocks into the rattle. Make a paper cap with slotted sides and glue it to the rattle opening. Secure it with a piece of string or a felt strip. Put a rubber band around the top glued parts overnight, until the glue has dried.

The Gourd Rattle (a papier mache' activity)

Materials: a small balloon, flour and water, strips of plain paper, stick, feathers, paint, beans.

1. Put beans etc. for rattle inside deflated balloon. Blow up the balloon to the desired size and knot end. Using cut 1" paper strips dipped in 1/4 c. flour and water, drape them around the balloon, completely covering it. Allow it to dry overnight. Paint the gourd and insert the handle.

Algonquins and Iroqouis had an ingenious array of rattles made from gourds, bark and the dew claws of hooved animals. Flutes and water drums also "propped up the song" with rhythm at ceremonies and diversions.

WAMPUM

WAMPUM

Materials: Graph paper cut the width and length of the belt (usually 2"– 4". Fine-tipped markers of purple, deep blue, violet, etc., pencil, and ruler for designing the belt.

Here are some important wampum belt designs. Each belt had value as money but, much more importantly, the belt signified a contract, a promise, or an important political event:

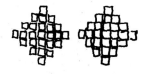

Diamonds mean
friendship

Squares mean
council fires

The circle means open and honest
talk. It represents the sun

Formation of the great
Iroquois League.
The tree is the Great
Tree of Peace

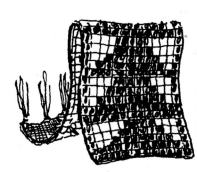

The Wing Belt was displayed
whenever the Iroquois
constitution was read. It
represents a pine tree
growing without limit

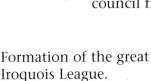

Holding hands honors a treaty
between two previous enemies

1. Decide on the design of the belt. Cut graph paper the length and width needed.
Cut a piece of crayon leather-treated paper to glue the belt on (see page 77).
2. Pencil in the design the first 2"- 3". Then color in with colored markers, leaving the white squares white. There are two methods:
    a. Color the squares with the lightest color, color over with darker, etc.
    b. Color each square a different color, all the dark purple first, next the blue, etc.
3. Add the ribbons and any decorative fringe when the
"wampum belt" is mounted.

Quanog and conch seashells were used for the white sections and the purple edges for the filler. The blue were the most important. Wampum means "strings of white" in Algonquin. The Onondaga chief Hiawatha mourned the death of his wife and daughters. He met the prophet Deganwida who consoled the grieving man with a string of white shells. Together they forged the League of Tribes.

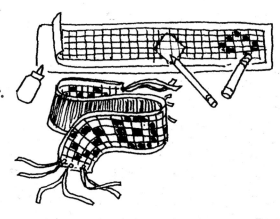

A MICMAC WOMAN'S HOOD

A Micmac Woman's Hood

Materials: *Two pieces of black or red construction paper 18" x 8", two strips of red paper 3" x 8" and an 18" x 2" strip, stapler, oil pastels of white, red, orange, dark blue, light blue, glue, scissors.*

1. Glue the red strips to either side of the black rectangles at the bottom leaving 1/2" of black paper on side and bottom edges.

2. Cut the two pieces of black paper at a diagonal of 9". This creates the peaked hat top.

3. The recurring design that was beaded or embroidered covering the surface of the hood is that of a stylized whale, lodges and canoe. This is the design:

4. Other beaded designs are:

5. Using a ruler and pencil measure the squares for the whale design and the other extra shapes and forms. The hood should be covered with the designs. The red border should be especially decorative.

6. Now color the pencil lines with oil pastels which show up nicely on the paper. Add a decorative edge.

7. Staple the back sides and front peak edges, back and front. Glue a 3/4" red paper strip along the edges, covering the staples.

Most Micmac women were wearing the peaked hoods by 1791. As early as 1611 it was recorded that "Micmac women were improving cloth with trim." All seams of cloth garments were outside and covered with a silk binding, usually red. It was thought the hoods may have been inspired by the French Brittany caps. Even today Micmac women make fine beaded and embroidered items for sale.

TWO WARRIOR'S FEATHERED HATS

Two Warrior's Feathered Hats

Feathers-in-Front Hat Worn by Abenaki of the Iroquois
Materials: Two feet by 4" band of brown school paper and red school paper,
oil pastels in white, blue, green, yellow, toothpick-porcupine quills, 15" x 18" white
school paper and brown, grey and black crayons or oil pastels for feathers, glue, string
or staple for closing band, pencil, ruler.

1. Measure the bands around the wearer's head size.
Adjust the red band to fit with a 2" overlap.
2. Look at the Woodland Indian pattern page 74.
Study the designs. Divide your red band into four
even sections with a pencil and ruler or by folding it
into four sections like an accordion. Pencil in the
design you choose. Go over your lines with oil pastels.
3. Cut the white paper into feather shapes with many
varying lengths. Look at the feathers in the photo.
4. Make a brown or black rib down the middle of
each feather and do slashes of black and brown color
to look like a turkey feather. Rub the colors together to
blend them. Make about 12 feathers.
5. Glue the decorated red band on the plain brown paper
band, **only gluing the bottom and side edges.** Lay the
band on a surface and stick the feathers between the brown and
red paper, choosing their arrangement. Glue them in place.
Lay some heavy books on the finished band where the
feathers have been glued for a few hours.

The Iroquois Gestowah (gesstah wah, a hat
with draping feathers)
Materials: Manila folder 22" x 2 1/2 " for headband
and circle with tabs and feathers, pattern on page 91,
the same feather materials, tape, stapler.
1. Measure and cut headband. Decorate headband with patterned band.
2. Cut 4 feathers for front, 2 for sides, 1 for middle, and 2 for back.
Color. Curve feathers backwards with a pencil so they will arch.
3. Look at the reduced gestowah pattern on page 91. Enlarge and
copy until the circle fits in the prepared headband. Make slots
with Exacto knife. Have an adult help with this step.
4. Staple circle tabs to headband so circle sits up at top of headband.
5. Insert feathers into slots and tape down with strong tape on the
bottom of the circle feather holder.

The Iroquois *gestowah* is an impressive ceremonial headdress which made its owner look
grand and important. Feathers from local birds would have been used such as turkey,
blue heron, eagle, partridge, hawk or crow.

THE MAKING OF THIRTEEN COLONIES

America has been a "melting pot" from the first decades of its colonial history. Explorers and settlers found the First Americans were organized into 300 different nations, spoke 143 languages and dialects, were different as well as similar to each other but in general were hunters, farmers and fisherman. The tragedy of three-fourths of the Indians succumbing to measles and smallpox in the first century left lands empty and seemingly "available."

The New Americans might be Russians who came with the Dutch to New Amsterdam. People from Poland arrived on the same ship as the English bound for Virginia. Early French trappers had been good at trading near the waterways for decades. Irish and Scotch mingled with Scandinavians with new settlements named after the birth country: New England, New Amsterdam, New Sweden, New Spain, etc.

In Europe intercountry travel was rare but in the New World there might be a Finnish community just a few miles from a Dutch town. Everyone shared holidays, traditions, skills and cultures. The Spanish settled New Mexico in 1610. The vaqueros, the original cowboys, herded the masses of cattle on the large ranches.

Big business has been an influence from the first colonial effort. The **Dutch West Indies Company** explored and settled much of what is New York. The **Plymouth Company** financed the Pilgrims' journey. The **Virginia Colony** supported Jamestown (hoping to find gold), and continued to fund future Virginia settlement efforts. Jamestown was settled in 1607 and abandoned by 1610. Lord de la Ware later tried a settlement again with 300 settlers.

The first boatload of seized Africans arrived in 1619. The plantation economy of tobacco needed intense labor. The hired Indians ran away when they became discontented and they knew the land well enough to make a successful escape. By 1658 there were hundreds of clearly established towns. There was a need for some order. It is clear that labor, too, struggled with the first strike by Polish glassmakers demanding the same rights as Englishmen. Throughout the 1600's boundaries were being drawn and surveys taken establishing specific colonies with historical names.

THE STORY OF THE THIRTEEN COLONIES

Massachusetts, 1620, is from an Algonquin word that means "at the big hill". In 1630 the first **purely Puritan** ship arrived with a charter from the king naming it Massachusetts Bay Colony. This allowed them to govern themselves.

Connecticut was named for the Mohican word *quinnitukqut*. Thomas Hooker was a minister near Boston. In 1633 he moved 100 people to the richer farmland of Connecticut. He had no charter and no claim on the land. He sent John Winthrop to England to get a charter from Charles II. The charter gave them the land that stretched as far as the Pacific Ocean.

Maine's and New Hampshire's northern lands were a gift from the king to John Mason and Ferdinando Gorges in 1623. They divided the land and Mason took New Hampshire (named after a county in England) and Gorges took Maine which remained part of Massachusetts until 1820 when it became a state.

Rhode Island was founded in 1636 by Roger Williams who preached total religious freedom. His views were so obnoxious to his fellow Bostonians that they banished him back to England. He fled into the wilderness and was saved by the Narragansett Indians and Powhatan, their sachem. Williams **bought** Rhode Island from the Indians. He developed Providence which welcomed Jews, Quakers, atheists and all beliefs (called riffraff by many.)

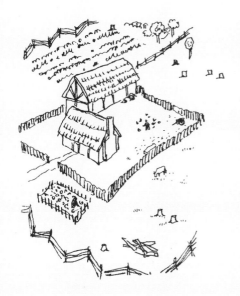

New York, 1624, was claimed by the Dutch after Henry Hudson sailed up his river. "Old Silver Nails", Peter Stuyvesant, ruled until 1664 when the British "bought" the land. The island had a wide street that ran end to end called "The Broad Way".

New Jersey, 1660 was a gift to George Carteret, who came from Jersey in England. The second gift from the Duke of York was to John Berkeley and it eventually became a royal colony.

Pennsylvania, 1647, means "Penn's woods" and was a gift to William Penn, whose father had loaned the king money. The king repaid the loan with a large gift of land in America. Penn was a devout Quaker and claimed the land for his Quaker faith. However, Penn invited all faiths to live there.

Delaware, 1634, was the land of the Lenni-Lape Indians. Johan Printz, called "Big Tub", was the Swedish governor of New Sweden, part of New Jersey and part of eventual Delaware. The leader of the second Jamestown was Lord de la Ware and his name became attached to this colony.

North and South Carolina were granted to eight lords by Charles II. They never lived in America; they just wanted to get rich raising grapes and selling wine, silk and olive oil. Instead indigo and rice became the best crops. Eventually both Carolinas became royal colonies: North Carolina in 1653 and South Carolina in 1670.

Virginia was first important with the settlement of Jamestown in 1607. Eventually it became a tobacco center and a slave-holding royal colony.

Maryland was settled by a Catholic, George Calvert (for the Virgin Mary), in 1634. The 1649 Toleration Act was a landmark law that promoted religious freedom...as long as you believed in God. If you were an atheist or a Jew...reconsider a move to early Maryland.

Georgia was planned by James Oglethorpe who wanted a place for people in debtor's prison to have a fresh start. Not many debtors were attracted by America's wilderness, but just about everybody else wanted to move to Georgia. By 1733 Georgia had become a royal colony with rich plantations and slaves and was under the king's government...not very close to Oglethorpe's original vision.

TWO THANKSGIVING FEAST FOODS

TWO THANKSGIVING FEAST FOODS

Materials: A batch of baking salt dough (the recipe on this page is better for this project than the other recipe on page 19) of 1 cup salt, 2 cups flour, 1 cup warm water, an oven, a cookie sheet, rolling pin, red, brown, white, black, yellow, orange paints, regular watercolor paint brush, dried corn, red, black, pinto beans, red hot candies, licorice stems, tools for incising dough such as a knife or nail. A straw for holes in the dough and a ribbon for hanging the turkey are optional.

Make the salt dough. The recipe for air-drying salt dough on page 19 is tougher to manipulate. This is a pliable, softer dough used by professional salt dough artists. Choose the recipe you wish to use depending on air drying the project or oven baking.

Turkey

1. Use a lump of salt dough the size of an orange. Roll it out to 1/4" thickness on a slightly floured surface. Cut it out with a dull knife around the pattern outline.
2. Have fun making the feathers from the excess dough (1/8" thick) or rolling the balls, adding beans corn, licorice cross-sections and red hots (the red hots will sometimes melt even at the lowest oven temp).
3. If you want to hang the turkey punch a hole with a straw 1" from the edge. Bake the turkey at 250 degrees for 3-5 hours. Check it periodically.
4. Paint with a watered palette so the incising shows: Choose your colors from browns, terra cotta, reds and oranges, yellows and black.

Lobster

There should be enough dough for the lobster. Look at pictures of the anatomy of this gourmet seafood. Follow the instructions for the turkey using a paint palette of red, terra cotta and black.

Traditionally the First Thanksgiving features the common turkey, and we know the Wampanoags and the early colonists did eat wild turkey. It is certain that seafood had to be a big part of the diet as well. It is recorded that lobsters were eaten so regularly the colonists tired of them. Mussels, clams, shrimp and other shellfish probably completed the menu.

STAND-UP PEOPLE

STAND-UP PEOPLE

Materials: Manila file folders, paper, crayons, water colors, oil pastels, colored pencils, markers or other coloring items, scissors, ruler, glue, patterns on pages 82-85.

1. Enlarge patterns to desired size (they are designed to be seven inches). Patterns are 65% in book.

2. Cut out file folder sandwich board rectangles. Cut out the front and back **on the fold**. With a ruler divide folder into three equal parts. Each part will be 3 7/8" wide and 8 1/4" long. Measure another line 7 1/2" long. The 7 1/2" line is the length of the sandwich board. The remaining strip will be inserted in the bottom of your sandwich board to hold it upright. Cut on lines to make three sandwich boards. Save three of the strips.

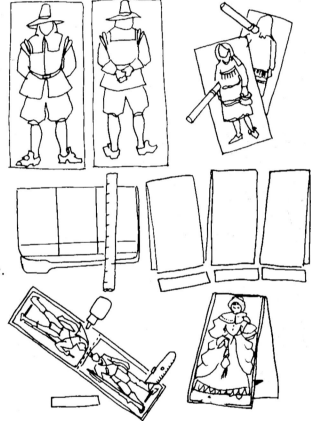

3. Color costumes front and back in correct colors. Create faces on the figures.

4. Glue front and back of person to folded rectangle.

5. Carefully, with adult supervision use an exacto knife to cut 1 1/2" slots about one inch up from cardboard bottom, center, front and back. Insert ends of strip through the slot to make the figures stand up.

The settlers of the New World, coming from many parts of Europe brought few treasures and usually only the clothes on their back. The Pilgrims and the Puritans were religious separatists and their standards of plain, simple fashion even led to laws forbidding the wearing of frills, laces and bright colors. The Quakers adopted even plainer attire. Natural dyes created rich blues, maroons and greens. Religious people did not just wear gray and black. Most clothing was made of handwoven, well-made fabrics meant to last a long time. Most colonists had a set of "good clothes" for special occasions. The beaver hat was in high fashion and a vital American export for over a hundred years. The French brought their sewing skills and regional styles of the rural provinces. By 1660 there were a thousand settlers in New Amsterdam eager for pretty clothes and accessories. The Germans, Swedish, Scotch and Irish tended to wear the peasant costumes of their homelands.

CHAP BOOK OF SANDPAPER PRINTS

Materials: Sandpaper squares (150 fine) 5" x 5", crayons or oil pastels, colored construction paper, white construction paper cut in 5" x 5" squares, newsprint, glue, an iron, plain scrap paper.

1. Choose as many alphabet letters as you have squares for. One square is for the letter, the second for the object drawing that begins with that letter.

2. Draw the full-size letter onto the sandpaper square. Then go over the letter with thick lines of crayon or oil pastel. The more crayon the better will be your sandpaper print. Fill the sandpaper square with color as a border, around and inside the letter, etc. Be sure to remember that the **letter of the alphabet** is your most important subject.

3. Place several layers of newspaper on a flat surface. Then put a plain piece of paper, then the paper square that you are going to transfer the print, and then another piece of plain paper.

4. Put the hot iron on the sandpaper print, making sure you go from corner to corner. Peel up an edge to check to see if the print is transferring. If it looks as though there is no transfer the sandpaper needs **much more crayon. You can add more crayon at any time.**

5. Remove the sandpaper and look at the print. Mount it on another piece of paper which is 5 1/2" x 5 1/2" so there is a border showing. Put these together in a chap book as students did in early Colonial days.

Children learned their first letters and numbers at home. Fine lettering and penmanship was a sign of good education. Youngsters were expected to practice their letters often. Wooden spelling blocks helped them learn the letters and practice making words. Horn books were made of wood, leather, cast lead and even ivory. The alphabet and numbers were on the paddle-looking objects. A piece of thin horn covered the letters as a protection. As horn books went out of style the game of shuttlecock became popular. Horn books were a handy paddle (battledores) and were either worn out or broken.

an early American garden

A WREATH OF NEW FOODS

A WREATH OF NEW FOODS

Materials: A pliable salt dough recipe of one cup salt, two cups flour, one cup warm water, an oven at 250 degrees, cookie sheet, knife, dough paste, acrylic paints, water, tiny brush, rolling pin, whole cloves.

This festive wreath in the Della Robbia style features the lifesaving agricultural foods that flourished in Indian gardens, decades before the colonists came to the New World. The three sisters, corn, beans and squash, were the staples. After corn, pumpkins were the staple crop. Beans of kidney, white and pinto were planted and Jerusalem artichokes, gourds, sunflowers and tobacco were part of the garden. Wild rice, chestnuts and berries were harvested too.

Wreath

1. Mix the salt, water and flour with a spatula. Give it a final 10 minute kneading with your hands, rolling it back and forth on a surface.

2. Roll the dough out on a cookie sheet surface to 1/4" thick. Put a circle template on top of the dough (ours was a plate 10" in circumference). Cut around the edge, placing the excess dough aside in a ball. Put a second circle carefully placed in the center and cut it out (ours was a 5" plate). Add the excess dough to the ball.

3. Make dough paste in a small bowl starting with a 1/2" ball and 1/2 teaspoon of warm water. Smash the water and dough with a fork until they create a paste. This is a "paste" for applying the dough foods. Apply to your dough with a brush to paste the dough foods.

New World Foods

Create the foods using these simple techniques with a knife and rolling oblong shapes, coils, many sizes of balls and flat, incised leaves. Try to cover the entire surface of the wreath. **Anytime you place a dough form on the wreath brush on dough paste as glue.** Insert a paper clip into dough at top for hanging. If you add the bottom label make four attaching holes with a straw. Bake at 250 degrees for 4-6 hours. Look at it from time to time, and when it starts to brown it is done. **Paint with a small brush and acrylic paints. Spray with a finish if desired.**

CORN HUSK TOYS

CORN HUSK TOYS

Materials: Twenty-three inches of dried tamale wrappers or dried corn husks, 20 ft. of twine, 15 inches of string, scissors, raffia, a pipe cleaner. Cattail leaves work best on the duck if they are available.

There is nothing original or fresh about this traditional children's activity as all Indian children have made these toys and taught their new colonial friends how to make them. The ducks were floated and raced on the streams and ponds.

Corn Husk Dolls

1. Soak the dried corn husks in warm water for about 10 minutes. Blot them dry. Gather twenty 10" lengths of twine. Tie an overhand knot at one end.
2. Trim the husks so they are about 8" long. Sandwich the knotted twine between the husks and tie at the base of the knot.
3. Make six strips of cut-up husk. Place a pipe cleaner with one set of strips and tie all but one end with string. Secure the end and braid the arms. Tie the end with string.
4. Take the body bundle and peel down the husks to create a head and expose the hair. Tightly tie the bundle where the neck should be, then insert the arms.
5. Braid another set of six husk strips twice to make two legs.
6. Insert the legs under the husks and tie them to the doll.
7. Snugly wrap a single husk around the doll's hips and tie it.
8. Braid the twine into two hair braids. Dress the doll by securing two or three husks around the waist upside down and tie with twine. Then peel down. Finally drape husks over the shoulders. Crisscross the ends in front and back and sash them around the waist with twine.

Corn Husk Duck (adapted from cattails)

1. You need about ten feet of dried corn husks laid end to end or long cat tail leaves. Overlay and wrap the presoaked husks until the duck's body is 4"– 5" in length and 2"– 3" in width. With three cut strips knot the duck's head at one end and insert it into the duck body. Tie the duck in two places with string or raffia or more corn husk strips.
2. When it is finished try floating it. If it tips adjust the head or thicken the dried body.

ROGER WILLIAMS BANNER

ROGER WILLIAMS BANNER

A group project: grades 5-9, 20 people

Materials: Resource materials with ample visuals on colonial life and Roger Williams, a linen-like fabric square 9" x 8", paper, pencils, colored pencils, fabric markers and fabric paint in most colors, brushes, water, background banner fabric of preferred size, UnderWonder iron-on fabric bonder, liquid fabric glue.

1. A list of 100 ideas is provided after a classroom study of Roger Williams. We suggest they are divided into the categories of Indians, Ideas, Events, Other. Resource materials are provided with visuals.

2. Each student chooses a topic and designs it on a 9" x 8" paper working *horizontally*. An Indian border from New England Indians frames the drawing.

3. After the drawing and border are approved color in with colored pencil.

4. Each student is given a fabric square to copy the pencil drawing onto the square.

5. Details are outlined in fabric markers. Most of the border detail is done with fabric markers.

If the student is doing a quote a watered-down colored wash is painted on the background. Beige, grey and light brown work well.

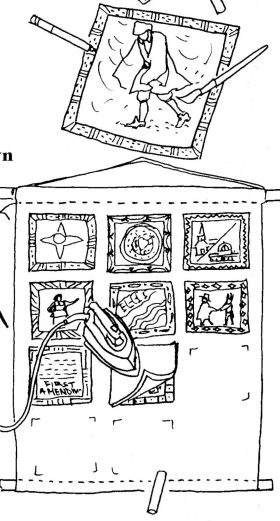

6. After the marker outlines and border have been completed the large patches of color such as grass, sky, ship hull, water, etc. are painted on with a diluted color. This has to be monitored because some students want vivid colors.

7. All quotes are lettered with student-preferred tools.

Assembling the banner (4' x 5' strong cotton)

1. Sew or glue a top and bottom 1" seam for a 1/2" piece of dowel for each. The background fabric measured 48" x 60" which allows for 15 - 20 squares. They are laid out on the fabric, measured carefully and marked with chalk. Two 2" strips of UnderWonder is put in place and with a piece of fabric or paper over the art iron the square onto the background fabric. Fabric glue may have to be used on corners.

2. Letter any title that you design as appropriate.

(Thank-you to Martha Ball's Butler Middle School geography classes who created the banner.)

Activity continued on page 78.

CARRYING BAG

"Indispensable" or Carrying Bag

Materials: A yard of plain light colored fabric, a hammer, access to several kinds of flowering plants, glue or staples, fabric pens (optional), big-eyed needle and colorful yarn.

1. Measure a circle on the fabric no smaller than 25"– 28". If you make a rectangle bag it should be 9" x 20". Only 9" x 8" will be decorated as the body of the bag with a 4" flap. Cut out your fabric.

2. Gather a few flowers. Be sparing in those you pick. Try your success on a piece of scrap fabric before you design your bag. You will be working with one petal at a time as you make your design. The flowers we carefully picked apart were: geranium petals, violets and violas, small pansies, vinca, tea roses, primrose, phlox and rock cress. Leaves that transferred well were bridal wreath, ferns and house ivy. Experiment, but remember that juicy parts do not work well. The fun is in experimenting.

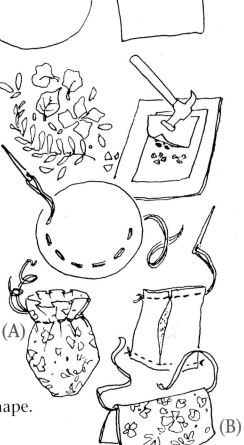

3. Cover a very hard surface like a sidewalk or wooden desk with protective papers. Place your fabric on the paper. Lay out three or four petals and leaves in a design in a 2"– 3" space. Put a protective paper over your design. Hammer the paper. Some of the plant color should come through. Gently lift your protective paper. How does it look? Hammer some more if you are not getting the petal or leaf shape. Continue on the entire piece until finished. It takes a while.

4. Put colorful yarn in a big-eyed needle and sew in and out 2" from the circle border, creating a drawstring. Pull it gently and you have a carrying bag. (A)

5. Make the rectangular bag (B) in the drawing by sewing the sides of the cotton rectangle (with hammered prints) with right sides together. Turn it right side out. Turn the flap over and finish the edges. A ribbon under the flap creates the attachment.

Colonial clothing did not have pockets. Women attached "indispensables" around their waists from a sash or belt that hung down at a convenient length. Care was taken to have these carrying bags pretty as well as useful. Ours have been made from pounding flower parts and leaves into patterns.

COLONIAL WEATHER VANES

COLONIAL WEATHER VANES

Materials: Two pieces of aluminum baking sheets 12" x 12", patterns, a bamboo skewer, straw, strong scissors, black paint or permanent marker, any other paint color, stapler, glue.

1. The materials listed are for one weather vane. Any symbol could be chosen such as a dog, sheep, cow, etc. Our samples were taken from the earliest colonial weather vanes.

2. Choose the symbol and draw it on the metal cookie sheet with a pencil. Cut it out with strong scissors that you don't mind dulling. If the subject is complicated, the cutting is tricky. The whale is very easy.

3. Trace around the first image and cut a second one as exact as it can be. Staple them together around the edges about 2" apart. ***Remember to keep a slot at the bottom for the skewer insert.***

3. Cut the skewer to measure 10". Cover the top 2" with glue and lift the metal foil and lay the glued skewer in place. Mold the metal around the skewer. Lay a heavy floppy book, such as a telephone book, on top of the glued section for several hours.

4. When the skewer has dried in place, paint or color it with marker. Then put it into a straw. Blow on it to make sure it turns with the wind. This can be stuck in dirt in gardens or attached to a railing. Be sure it has space to turn.

Colonial weather vanes have become sought-after collectors items. If you travel around the New England states you notice that *every* rooftop and cupola has a whimsical weather vane...some you are told are several generations old. Often the weather vane gave a hint of the owner's name (such as Gardner) or the kind of work that was done on the farm.

PAPER CHAINS

Paper Chains

Materials: Colored paper, scissors, pencil, glue or tape, patterns on page 75.
Paint and markers optional.

1. Cut the paper into sections 5"– 7"
wide and as long as needed.

2. Fold your paper strip accordion-
style into three to four sections. For a
longer paper chain add more paper
strips. Cutting this many is about the
best a scissors can cut.

3. Choose a pattern from the pattern
page or design your own.

4. If you want to color or paint your
paper, do it now. Suggestions are to
cut some out of wrapping or wall-
paper or sponge paint some with
color dabs. Let the paper strip dry
before proceeding.

5. Refold your dry paper strip. *Trace
the design onto your folded paper strip,
making sure the design extends to the
folded sides so that when it is cut out
the shapes* **are connected.**

6. Secure your paper for cutting by
slipping a paper clip onto a section
which will be cut away.

7. Repeat as many of the same or different designs as you
wish. Fasten ends of your paper chains together with tape or glue.

Paper chains make decorative edges for bulletin boards and other displays.
Each pattern could be used for the front of an invitation or a personal card.
If you create a theme holiday evergreen tree the paper chains can be strung
from the branches. The Early American people figures on page 82–85 could be
hung from branches as well. A paper chain single makes a nice book
marker or can be used as a stencil for wrapping paper or for some traditional
Colonial decorating.

CULTURAL PATTERNS

VIKING

INDIAN

QUILL WORK

BEADWORK

MOOSEHAIR EMBROIDERY

BIRCH BARK DECORATION

COLONISTS

A B C D E F
& 1 2 3 4 5 6

SAMPLER EMBROIDERY

BEAD WORK

FURNITURE PAINTING

PAPER CHAIN PATTERNS

ARCHITECTURE IN THE NEW WORLD

Early American architecture for both Indians and colonists was a combination of their traditions and materials they had at hand. Indian homes were made of saplings in natural arched and conical shapes which were covered with bark. Colonial homebuilders used natural materials like bark, stone and thatch and added European engineering elements of sawed boards, molded bricks, and post and beam construction.

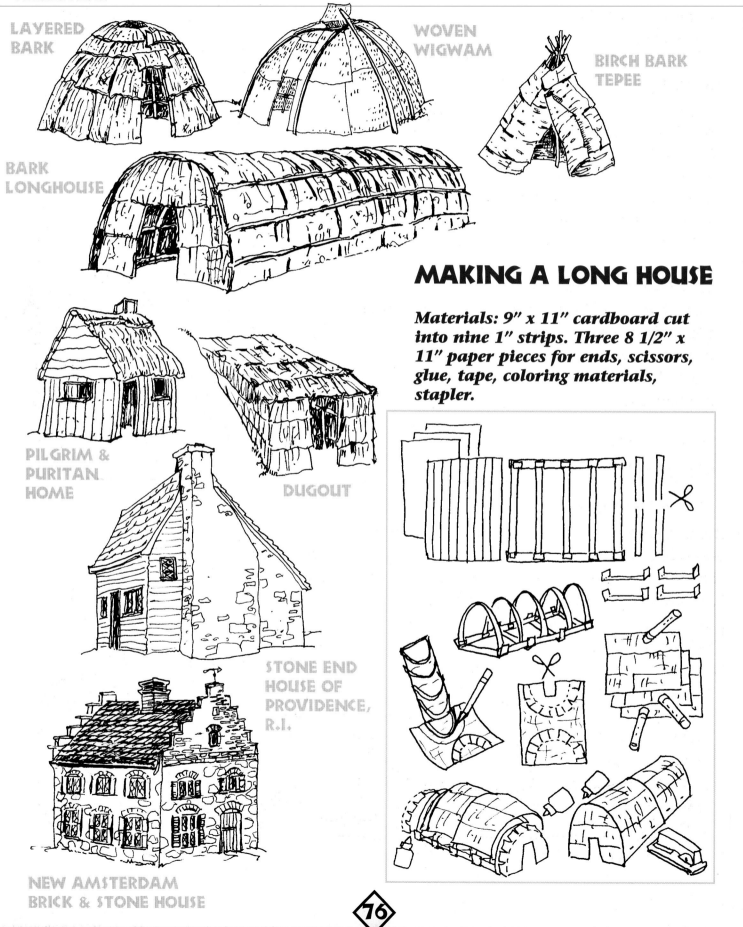

LAYERED BARK

WOVEN WIGWAM

BIRCH BARK TEPEE

BARK LONGHOUSE

PILGRIM & PURITAN HOME

DUGOUT

STONE END HOUSE OF PROVIDENCE, R.I.

NEW AMSTERDAM BRICK & STONE HOUSE

MAKING A LONG HOUSE

Materials: 9" x 11" cardboard cut into nine 1" strips. Three 8 1/2" x 11" paper pieces for ends, scissors, glue, tape, coloring materials, stapler.

FAKING IT WITH ART

Creating a "birch bark" surface
It is always preferred to have a piece of real birch bark in front of the artist to do the best simulation.

To give plain white paper or manila card stock the buff texture of bark is a color-and-rub process. Always experiment first on a small scrap paper.

1. Using ocher, yellow, brown, white **oil pastels** (the best) or crayons color the paper all over. Yellow and ocher should be dominant, next brown. With four finger pads rub the colors together.

2. Looking at the photograph of bark things, randomly add the brown bark-lines. Streak a little white through the lines.

Creating a "buckskin" surface
If you have a piece of tanned hide it would help with the authentic product.

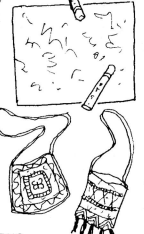

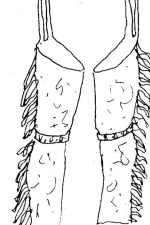

Color the paper with ocher, white and yellow oil pastels or crayons or both. Rub them together until blended.

Create an "antler" or "bone" surface using this technique, pale colors, and cardboard.

---

continued from page 13

Helmet of Foil with Gold and Brass Trim
Materials: Aluminum cookie sheet 10" x 15", triangle and visor pattern pieces, yellow and orange permanent markers, hole punch, scissors, pencil, stapler.

Cut 3 triangles from cookie sheet. Cut 1 triangle that is cut in half. You have 5 triangle shapes. Cut visor from pattern. Cut out 1 strips (as many as you can) from remaining foil. Cut 2 foil eyebrows using scrap paper. Color the eyebrows with orange marker. Color the strips and visor with yellow marker. Assemble the triangles by overlapping edges and stapling. Use the 3 biggest triangles for front. Use the 2 smaller for the back. Try on your helmet for size. Staple "gold" bands over seams. Cut holes with hole punch in the front band and the "brass" eyebrows. Staple the visor onto the front of helmet, then staple the eyebrows.

Birch Bark Art continued from page 43

1. Cut three matching shapes allowing for a 1" connecting edge on each.
2. Incise your design with a nail point as described in the first two projects.
3. Score down the edge of each box, fold the edge and glue each side.
4. Stand the triangle cylinder on birch cardboard and cut two triangles to fit the top and bottom, allowing for a 1/2" edge.
5. Score the final shape and turn up the edges, cutting the excess corners. Glue the bottom in place to fit.
6. Punch with a scissors point two holes 1" apart on the lid. Pull through a yarn or leather handle and knot or glue in place. Glue down edges and place lid snugly inside the box top.

Scratching designs into bark was an old tradition with the Wabanaki Indians in Maine and New Brunswick. A Passamaquoddy man named Tomah Joseph became a master of this craft technique. He adapted the age-old art into items popular with tourists for decades. He sold his wares at Campobello Island, and it is easy to imagine that probably the Roosevelt family saw them. He was a summer fishing guide, a storyteller, a traditional dancer, and a hunter and fisherman. He died in 1914, having published his stories and placed his bark art in collections. His son and grandson have carried on his tradition.

Wrapped Hair Lock continued from page 27

1. Cut a 4 foot hank of 20 yarn strands. Wrap it with colorful yarn, feathers, beads, etc. Make a silver conch out of aluminum sheeting. Coil it at the top of the black paper cross band and staple in place. Staple it down the strip and have it hang decorously down the back.

The "roach" is called a "Mohawk" today but many Indian men of several tribes wore one. It took several porcupines to create a full roach. Smaller roaches were made from strips of deerhide with the hair still on it. Some Indians shaved their scalps and kept a scalp strip of long hair. They attached the roach to it. Women and men wore braids. Some resources say the long scalp lock was a sign of a warrior, especially with the Iroquois. There are early drawings of warriors in body paint with the long hair lock.

Roger Williams Banner continued from page 67

Roger Williams was born in London in 1603. He attended Cambridge and became a minister in the Puritan faith. Because of the persecution of the Puritans he joined the thousands that fled to America. His strong, unwavering beliefs of "soul Liberty" that all people should have total religious freedom caused him to be banished from Boston in 1636. He fled into the winter wilderness for several weeks where he was befriended and saved by the Narraganset Indians. He bought the land for Rhode Island and built Providence on the shore. He welcomed atheists, Jews, Quakers and all people to his flourishing town. He operated a trading fort and never sold alcohol or guns to the Indians. He was a close friend to Powhatan and all Indians considered him a trusted friend. He negotiated several treaties but could not avoid the King Philip's War of 1675-76 which massacred the Narragansets and burned much of Providence including his own property.

ACKNOWLEDGEMENTS OF GRATITUDE
Jerome Kelley, a Western Abenaki elder who advised us on that aspect of the book
Terri Clothey, a Micmac and owner of the shop *A Different Path* in Littleton, New Hampshire
also helped us with information.

BIBLIOGRAPHY

THE VIKINGS

Clare, John D., *The Vikings: Living History,* Gulliver Books, New York, 1992.

Clarke, Helen, *Vikings: The Civilization Library,* Gloucester Press, London, 1979.

Gibson, Michael, *The Vikings, The Wayland Documentary History Series,* London, 1972.

Streissguth, Thomas, *Life Among the Vikings: The Way People Live,* Lucent Books, San Diego, 1958.

Time-Life Series, *Vikings: Raiders from the North,* New York, 1993.

Tryckvare, Tre, *The Vikings,* Crescent Books, New York, 1972.

Wilson, David M., *The Vikings,* British Museum Press, London, 1987.

Wooding, Jonathan, *The Vikings,* Rizzoli International Publications, New York, 1996.

THE NEW ENGLAND INDIANS

Johnson, Michael G. and Richard Hook, *American Woodland Indians,* Men-At-Arms Series,
    Osprey Publishing, United Kingdom.

Wilbur, Keith C. *The Woodland Indians,* The Illustrated Living History Series, Globe Pequot Press,
    Old Saybrook, Connecticut, 1995.

Wilbur, *The New England Indians,* The Illustrated Living History Series, Globe Pequot Press,
    Old Saybrook, Connecticut, 1995.

Isaacs, Sally Senzell, *America in the Time of Pocahontas, 1590-1754,* Heineman Library,
    Des Plaines, Illinois, 1998.

Green, Rayna, *Women in Indian American Society,* Chelsea House, New York, 1992.

Murdoch, David, *North American Indian,* Eyewitness Books, Knopf, New York, 1995

Miller, Jay, *American Indian Games,* Children's Press, New York, 1947.

Haslam, Andrew and Alexandra Parsons, *North American Indians,* Thomson Learning, England, 1995.

Sonneborn, Liz, *Native American Culture,* Rourke Publications, Vero Beach, Florida, 1994.

Weatherford, Jack, *Indian Givers,* Crown Publishing, New York, 1988.

Russell, *Indian New England Before the Mayflower,* Hanover, New Hampshire, 1980.

Hunt, W. Ben, *The Complete How-to book of Indian Craft,* Macmillan, New York, 1973.

Newman, Dana, *The Woodland Indians,* Prentice Hall, New Jersey, 1997.

THE SEVENTEENTH CENTURY OF COLONIAL LIFE

Sloan, Eric, *Sketches of America Past,* Promontory Press, New York, 1986.

Sloan, *Diary of an American Boy,* Promontory Press, New York, 1986.

Sloan, *ABC Book of Early Americana,* Doubleday, Garden City, New York, 1963.

Welcome to Felicity's World, The American Girl Collection, Pleasant Co., Middleton, WI., 1999.

Welcome to Addy's World, The American Girl Collection, Pleasant Co., Middleton, WI., 1999.

Bowen, Gary, *My Village, Sturbridge,* Farrar, Strauss and Giroux, New York, 1977.

Life in Colonial America, Deerfield Museum, 1994.

Fisher, Margaret and Mary Jane Fowler, *Colonial America,* Gateway Press, Inc., Michigan, 1988.

Masoff, Joy, *Colonial Times, 1600 to 1700,* Chronicles of America, Scholastic, New York, 2000.

Egger-Bovet, Howard and Marlene Smith-Baranzi, *USKids History, Book of the American Colonies,*
    Little Brown and Co.,Yolla Bolly Press, Covelo, CA, 1996.

Hakim, Joy, *Making Thirteen Colonies, 1600-1740,* History of Us, Oxford Univ. Press, New York, 1993.

Hakim, Joy, *The First Americans, History of Us,* Oxford Univ. Press, New York, 1993.

INDEX

Hands-on Alaska
(ISBN 0-9643177-3-7)

Hands-on America Vol. I
(ISBN 0-9643177-6-1)

Hands-on Rocky Mountains
(ISBN 0-9643177-2-9)

Hands-on Latin America
(ISBN 0-9643177-1-0)

Books from
KITS
PUBLISHING

Consider these books for:
the library • teaching social studies
art • multicultural programs
ESL programs • museum programs
community youth events • home schooling

Hands-on Celebrations
(ISBN 0-9643177-4-5)

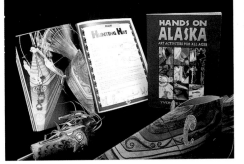

Hands-on Pioneers
(ISBN 1-57345-085-5)

Hands-on Africa
(ISBN 0-9643177-7-X)

Hands-on Asia
(ISBN 0-9643177-5-3)

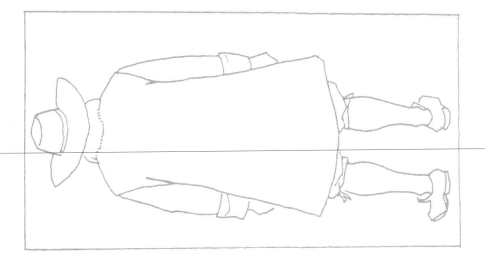

Quaker

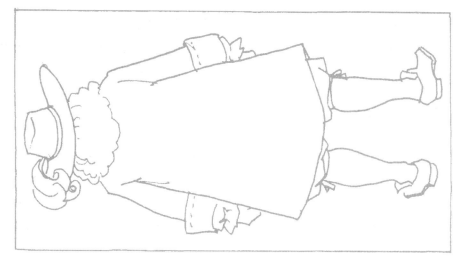

Merchant

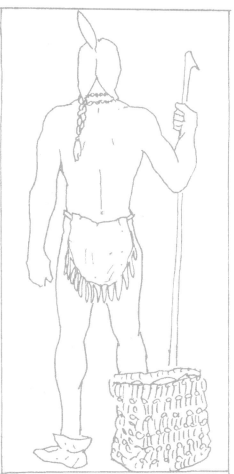

Wampanoag

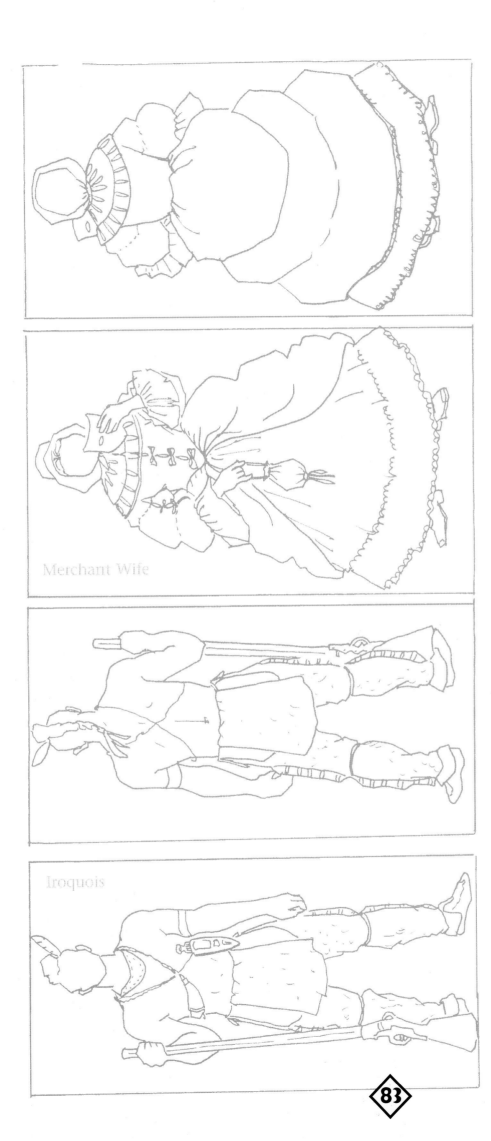

Merchant Wife

Iroquois

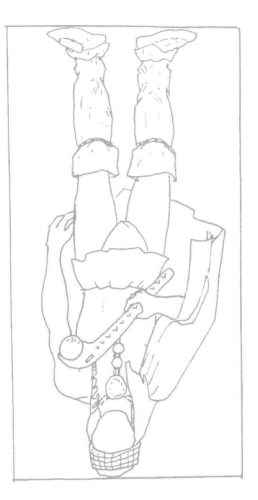

Narraganset

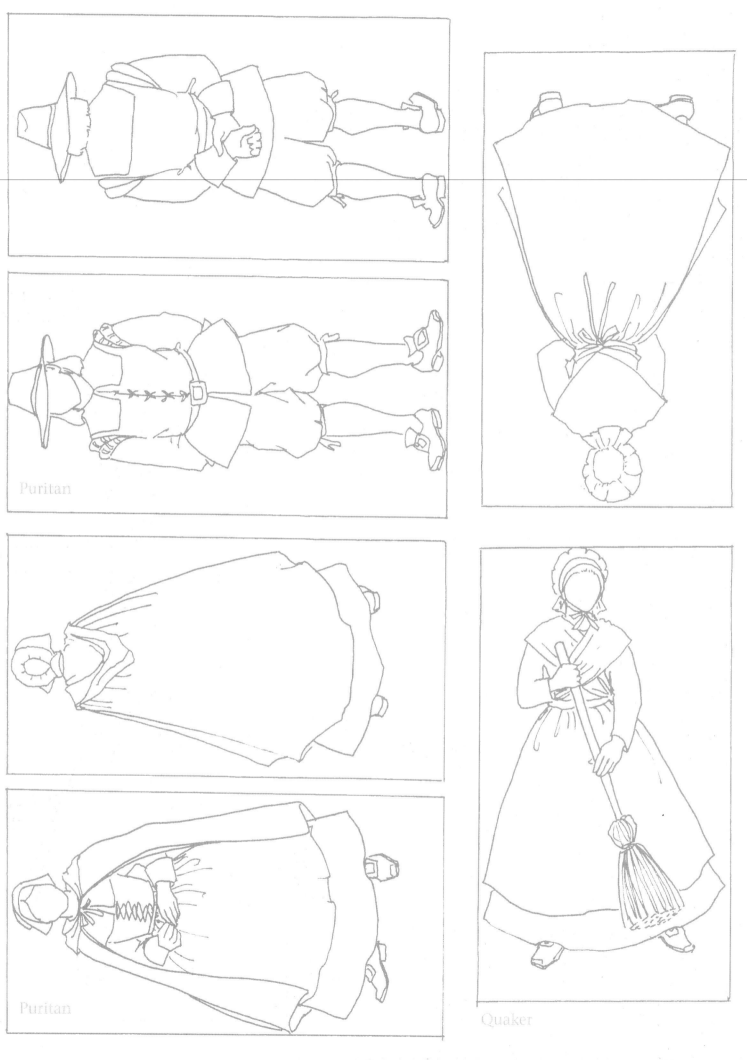

Puritan

Puritan

Quaker

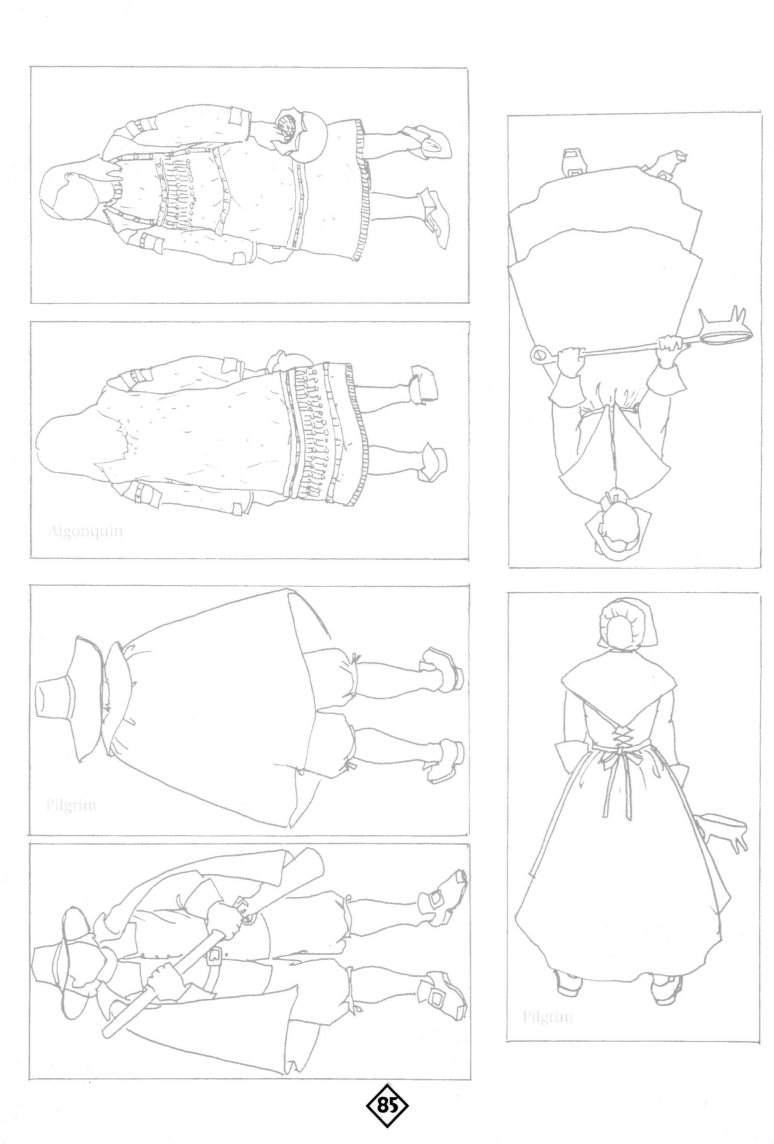

Algonquin

Pilgrim

Pilgrim

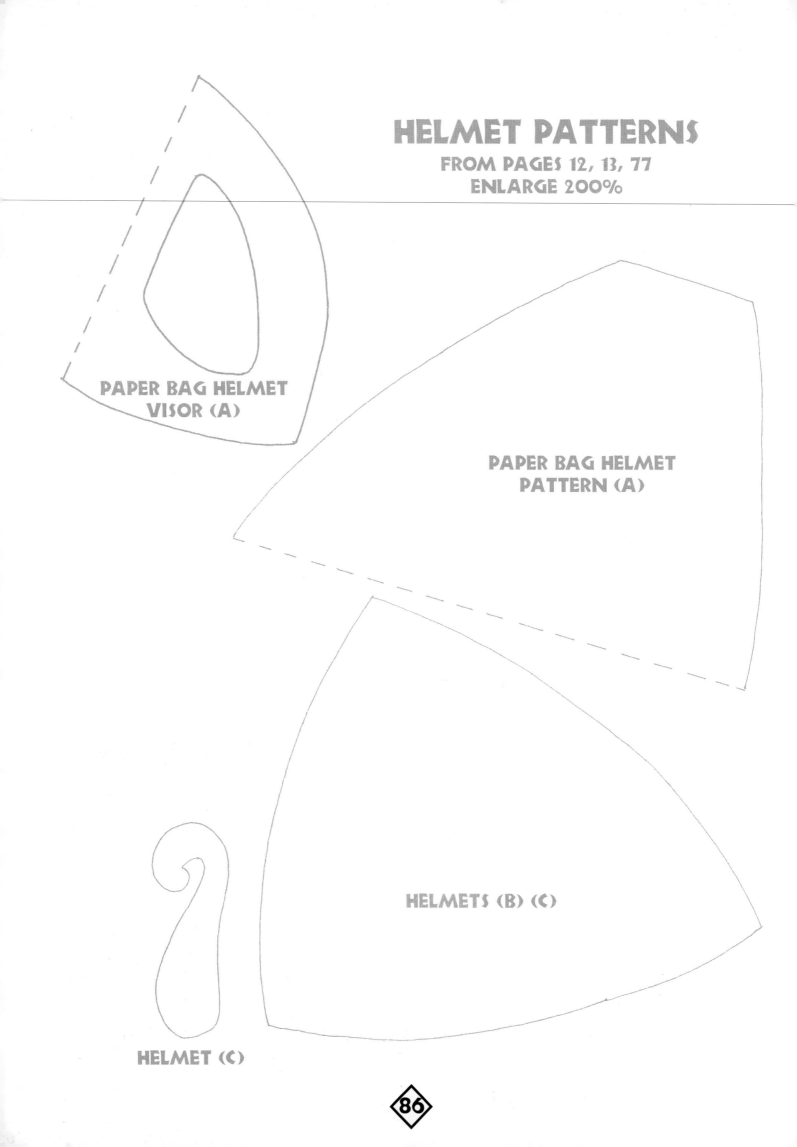

HELMET PATTERNS
FROM PAGES 12, 13, 77
ENLARGE 200%

PAPER BAG HELMET
VISOR (A)

PAPER BAG HELMET
PATTERN (A)

HELMETS (B) (C)

HELMET (C)

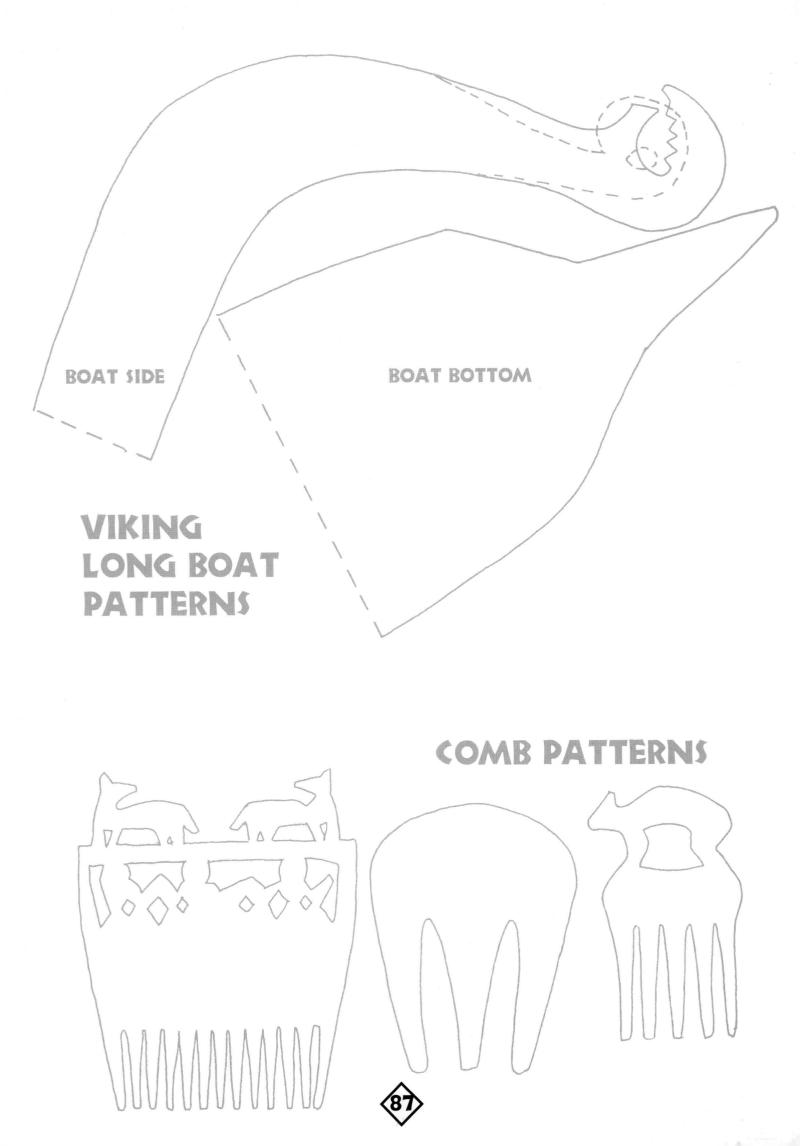

BOAT SIDE

BOAT BOTTOM

VIKING LONG BOAT PATTERNS

COMB PATTERNS

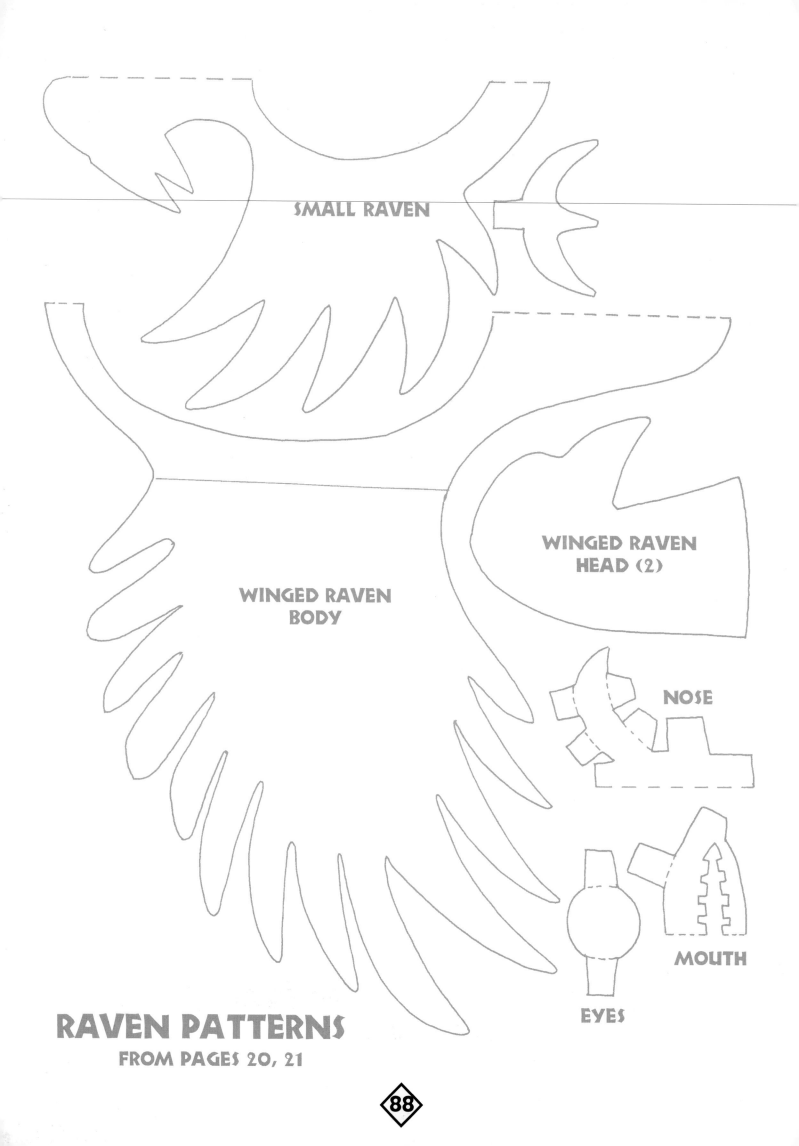

SMALL RAVEN

WINGED RAVEN
HEAD (2)

WINGED RAVEN
BODY

NOSE

MOUTH

EYES

RAVEN PATTERNS
FROM PAGES 20, 21

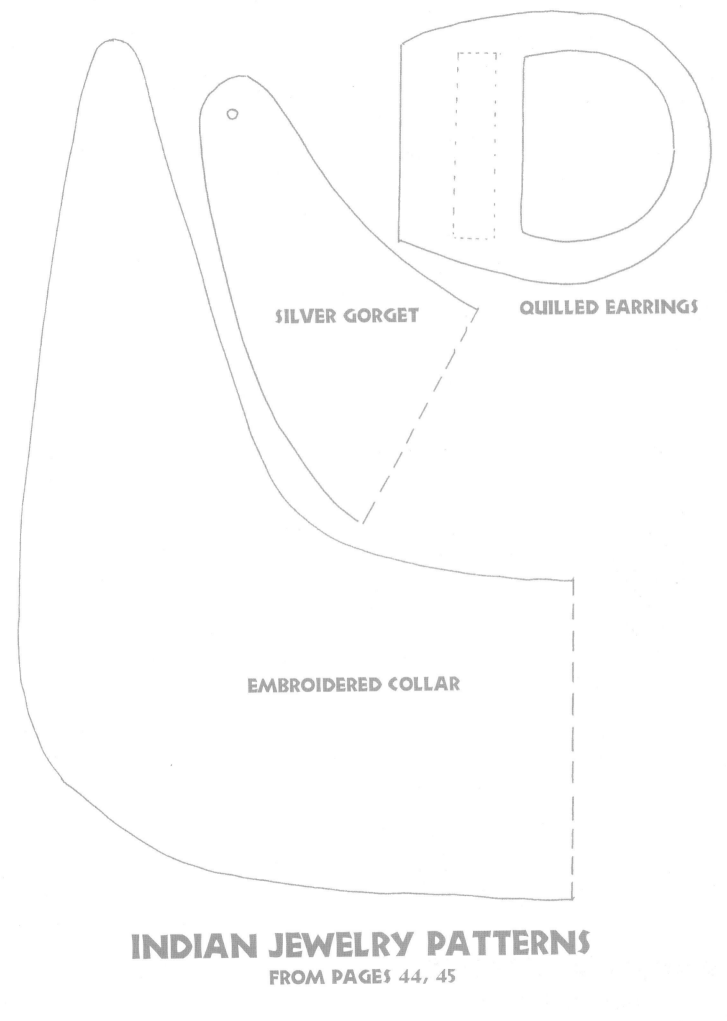

SILVER GORGET

QUILLED EARRINGS

EMBROIDERED COLLAR

INDIAN JEWELRY PATTERNS
FROM PAGES 44, 45

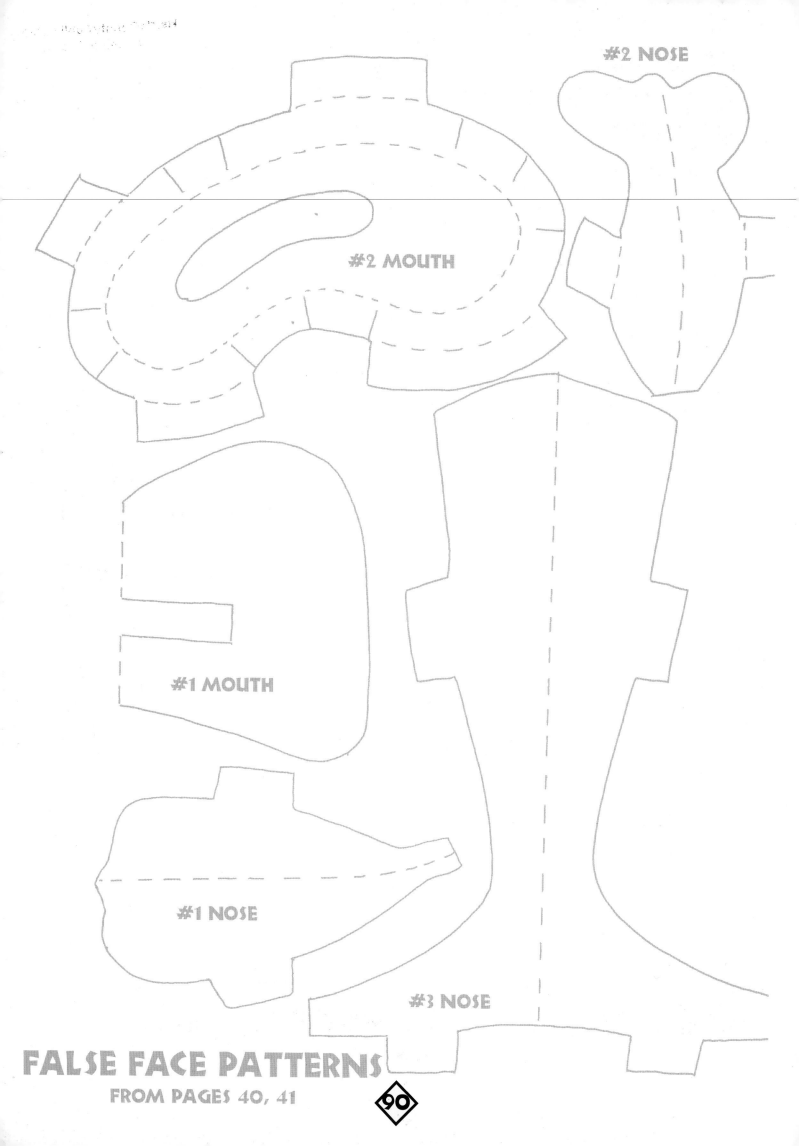

#2 NOSE

#2 MOUTH

#1 MOUTH

#1 NOSE

#3 NOSE

FALSE FACE PATTERNS
FROM PAGES 40, 41

MUSICAL
INSTRUMENTS
PATTERNS
FROM PAGES 46, 47

**RATTLE
TOP**

ANKLE RATTLE

**BIRCH BARK
RATTLE**

IROQUOIS GESTOWAH

REDUCED FEATHERED HAT PATTERNS
FROM PAGES 52, 53

WEATHER VANE PATTERNS
FROM PAGES 70, 71

HEAD

TURTLE PATTERNS REDUCED
FROM PAGES 30, 31

BOTTOM

TOP